"But he was shooting at you!"

"Yes," Quent explained to Cassie. "But it goes with the territory. It's part of the job. And I know what I'm doing, believe it or not."

"I didn't say you didn't!" Cassie's voice rose to match his. "I hate this." She gestured into the air, feeling the truth that she'd held secret for so long finally coming out. "I'm terrified that something will happen to you. I hate it. I'm so afraid. I—I'm sorry."

His arms went around her, supporting her as she leaned against his chest. She loved him, but she couldn't ruin his life by marrying him. She'd be a burden. He'd know her fear.

Then he shook her, forcing her to look up at him. "Cassie," he said, "it's okay. I understand about your fear. We can face it together."

Dear Reader,

Welcome to Silhouette. Experience the magic of the wonderful world where two people fall in love. Meet heroines who will make you cheer for their happiness, and heroes (be they the boy next door or a handsome, mysterious stranger) who will win your heart. Silhouette Romances reflect the magic of love—sweeping you away with books that will make you laugh and cry, heartwarming, poignant stories that will move you time and time again.

In the next few months, we're publishing romances by many of your all-time favorites, such as Diana Palmer, Brittany Young, Emilie Richards and Arlene James. Your response to these authors and other authors of Silhouette Romances has served as a touchstone for us, and we're pleased to bring you more books with Silhouette's distinctive medley of charm, wit and—above all—*romance*.

I hope you enjoy this book and the many stories to come. Experience the magic!

Sincerely,

Tara Hughes
Senior Editor
Silhouette Books

CURTISS ANN MATLOCK
For Each Tomorrow

Silhouette Romance

Published by Silhouette Books New York

America's Publisher of Contemporary Romance

Special thanks to Gary Hensley
and Mr. and Mrs. Dakota Cagle.

SILHOUETTE BOOKS
300 E. 42nd St., New York, N.Y. 10017

ISBN: 0-373-08482-X

First Silhouette Books printing January 1987

America's Publisher of Contemporary Romance

Printed in the U.S.A.

Books by Curtiss Ann Matlock

Silhouette Special Edition

A Time and a Season #275
Lindsey's Rainbow #333

Silhouette Romance

Crosswinds #422
For Each Tomorrow #482

CURTISS ANN MATLOCK

loves to travel and has lived in eight different states, from Alaska to Florida. Sixteen years ago she married her high-school sweetheart and inspiration, James. The Matlocks are now settled in Oklahoma, where Curtiss is concentrating on being a homemaker and writer. Other time is taken up with gardening, canning, crocheting, and of course, reading. She says, "I was probably born with a book in hand."

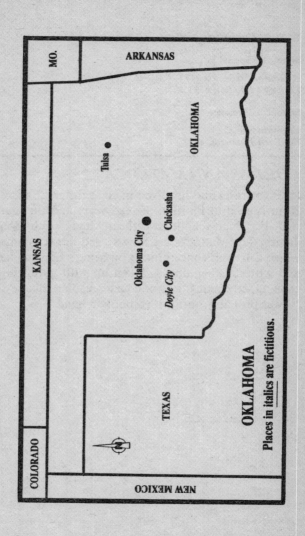

OKLAHOMA

Places in italics are fictitious.

Chapter One

Memories. They floated through Cassie Marlow's mind, some warm as the sun shining brightly through the windshield, others flighty and unpredictable as the breeze which whipped through the open window.

Memories were a mystery, she mused, giving the phenomenon deliberate consideration as she squinted in the bright light. When there was something a person needed to remember, the thought would escape, and when one would rather let go of past incidents, the memory returned unbidden to haunt and taunt. Memories were life in a way, she supposed, made up of things sweet and warm, as well as sour and cold.

Her memories of Quentin Hatfield fell into both of these categories, she decided as she turned the pickup from the blacktop and headed down a sandy-clay road.

Quentin Hatfield had been away for nine years. Oh, he'd come home to visit his family and friends, but Cassie had never seen him. Mostly by choice—hers, she knew, and his, too, she suspected. But now he'd come home to stay, to work as a ranger alongside her brother, and she'd more than likely be seeing him often. So she'd decided now was as good a time as any to drop by where she knew he'd be and get the greeting over with, and also satisfy her curiosity.

The air was crisp for early October, but the sky was wide and blue, reminding Cassie of a time nine years ago. This memory came sweet and warm. That day, too, had been cloudless, but simmering with summer heat. She smiled inwardly, feeling again the heat of that day. How strange memory was to be so strong and vivid. She could almost smell the heat, and the image of Quentin Hatfield's bobcat-colored eyes shimmered before her.

It was a time a woman would remember, she supposed.

But it had been a long time ago.

Ahead, at the side of the road, sat several pickups, and pulling her own behind them, Cassie slipped from the seat. She didn't see her brother Springer's truck, but the breeze brought the sound of rough male voices and laughter, attesting that there was a gathering in the meadow over the hill.

She paused for a moment, thinking of why she was there. It was normal, healthy, human curiosity. After all, she'd grown up with Quent, he'd been like one of her brothers, and she hadn't seen him in nine years. It was perfectly human, she told herself, to wonder about him and want to see him now.

Yet embarrassment lingered. How odd after all these years. But they had parted feeling somewhat ill at ease. It had been a jolt to find out that the boy whom she'd always thought of as a brother wasn't brotherly anymore, and that he'd become a man.

Quentin Hatfield had been the first man to make her see herself as a woman. And it had shocked him as well as her, she thought with an inner chuckle. Turning her face to catch the light breeze, she again remembered that hot, sunny day. In actuality she hadn't thought about it in years, not until she learned that Quent was returning.

And yet she hadn't forgotten his kiss.

Would Quent remember? she wondered as she started up the entrance to the pasture, walking in long lithe strides, her hands snuggled into the pockets of her light jacket. She hesitated for a second. Would he say anything about that day? Oh, Cassie, don't be silly, she scolded herself, tossing her long thick ponytail back from her shoulder. No doubt Quent had kissed many women since then.

She reached the top of the entrance and hesitated, scanning the scene before her, the usual impromptu Saturday gathering of old friends. Automatically she took in the weathered wooden corral in the wide corner of the pasture and the men standing around it. Her brother Springer caught her sight first. He sat upon the top rail of the corral. The tallest of the tall, two-hundred-plus pounds, his brown Stetson bright in the sunlight, he wasn't a man one missed. Several pickups were parked to the side. Springer's was among them, with a cooler full of beer, no doubt, she thought as two men reached into it and lifted out cans. Three horses grazed lazily nearby, their tails flipping softly, ears twitching at the sound of the good-humored hollering that was going on.

Cassie recognized the familiar scene as she walked easily toward the group, her gaze searching, though she carefully appeared not to. She knew the men, as well as the two women among them. Several glanced her way, nodding an easy greeting.

She saw Quent before he saw her. His profile was striking as he leaned against the corral rail, talking. He was tall, taller than she'd remembered, and still very lean. Though his hair was darker, and he now wore a very thick and handsome mustache, he was easily recognizable—that set of his shoulders, the supple grace with which he stood. And of course, though there were only two other women there, one stood by his side.

As her heart picked up tempo, she scolded herself for silliness. Good grief, she'd known Quentin Hatfield since she was three.

"'ello, Cassie," Hadley Smith said as she came to a stop next to the corral. His weather-beaten face broke into a wide grin of pleasure.

A ranger, he'd been a close friend of her father's, and like an uncle to her and her brothers. At the moment he wore his uniform, minus his gun, and it was a mass of wrinkles as usual. Although he was an older man, his gaze flicked quickly downward before finding her face again. Most men did that to her. She'd grown used to it and took no offense.

"Hello, Hadley." She looked around the corral in a fashion of friendly interest, and her gaze was drawn again to Quent then swung quickly away. "What's going on?"

"Oh," Hadley drawled, "these young fellers are just out for a lazy afternoon of fun. They're trying to decide who should brave this critter here."

He nodded in the direction of what Cassie had assumed to be a bull. Her thoughts had been preoccupied, and she hadn't looked directly at the animal at the far end of the corral, but she did now. She opened her mouth, then shut it.

The animal was a bull all right—a buffalo bull.

"They're not?" she said.

Hadley simply grinned and nodded. "Your brother Springer's been at it already, trying to put a hat on the darn thing."

"You should stop it, Hadley," Cassie said, eyeing the nervous bull. It was Hadley's ranch, and at middle age, with a good many experiences behind him as a ranger and rancher, he had the respect of the other younger men, such as her brother.

"They're just having some fun, Cassie. And maybe they'll learn a valuable lesson or two." His crinkled eyes held a mischievous twinkle.

No doubt, Cassie thought, several of the men ringing the corral didn't truly know much about buffalo. But she did, and Springer should. They'd had two one summer, when they'd thought of investing in the beefalo market before they'd had the good sense to finally get rid of the troublesome beasts. It was probably that experience with the buffalo that led her brother into his antics now—the challenge and danger of it.

Perhaps not everyone found the animal as stubborn and ornery as she had, but that was her opinion still. The animals tended to look harmless enough, but they were so powerful that a barbed wire fence couldn't hold them. If they chose, they could go through it as if it weren't there, and often did the same to rail fencing. They were protective of the cows and calves of the herd, and once riled, there was no telling what they might do. When they had tried to load their buffalo into the cattle trailer to be sold, the male had simply gone in to come out at the side, heedless of the absence of a door.

Concern nibbled at Cassie as she looked from the buffalo to her brother. They were both quite large, certainly equal in stubbornness and unpredictability, but she wouldn't put odds on which one would win, should they charge each other.

"Hey, Cassie!" Springer called, seeing her just at that moment.

She smiled in greeting, her gaze slipping past him to Quent, curiosity and anticipation churning harder inside. At that moment Quent, too, turned at the call, and his gaze met hers. A surprising warmth seemed to touch her. *Did his gaze linger?*

"Quent," Springer was calling, "come on over and see Cassie."

It had been so long, and they'd grown up together, watched *Lassie* together, swam together, and once even shared the same piece of chewed gum. She knew the man intimately, yet he was a stranger.

It was odd how in one instant all this would flit through her mind, along with the lingering memory of a warm summer afternoon when they'd each discovered they were not actually brother and sister. And the question occurred to her again—did he remember?

Schooling her expression carefully, she pushed away from the corral fence and went to meet him. She wasn't one of the hundred females of the area who was dying to meet Quentin Hatfield. He was an old friend, like a brother.

"Hello, Quent," she said, pleasure slipping into her smile. "It's good to see you."

"Hello, Cassie." His voice was deeper than she remembered. But he'd always said her name in that way, sort of drawing it out. "How about a hug for an old friend?"

Before she could answer, he wrapped his arms around her, hugging her firmly against his chest. With a natural instinct she hugged him in return. The muscles of his waist and back were hard and lean beneath her hands, and he smelled faintly of musky cologne and sweat and fresh fall air. It was good to see him, she thought, such an old and dear friend. So many years had passed.

Letting her go, he stepped away, though still keeping hold of her hand.

His thick hair was shorter, though the same brown, burnished in the sunlight. His mustache was the same color, if perhaps tinged more with red. His eyes were the same soft golden-brown, yet they were different, older. As she watched, they flickered with amusement, then widened as he surveyed her in like manner, his gaze moving over her face, slipping downward, then back up.

"Good grief, Springer," Quent said. "Your big sister has grown up."

"You haven't seen her in nine years." Springer laughed over his shoulder as his attention was drawn back to the corral, and he started yelling challenges to a friend.

"No, I haven't," Quent remarked, his gaze warm and thoughtful upon her face.

Cassie looked to his eyes for the memory, but she couldn't tell. "I was eighteen," she quipped, almost wishing she hadn't said it, thinking that it alluded to the time she really didn't want to speak of.

"Well, we've all aged since then." Again he gave his mellow smile.

His gaze moved over her body, lingering just slightly at her breasts. She knew the look. All three of her brothers, and Quent as well, had always had a look they reserved for women. It was easy and daring and flirting, all at the same time. Because of her experience, she chuckled now and slipped her hand from his. A thought pricked at her, hardly noticed among all the others—Quent had never looked at her that way. And curiously, she realized she'd never felt so feminine in all her life.

Turning from him, she walked to the corral, extremely conscious of her movements and of Quent stepping close beside her. Leaning her arms on the top rail, she watched as one of the men tried his hand at flopping a hat on the skittish buffalo. She felt Quent's gaze.

"Springer says you're running the store on your own now," he said.

Cassie nodded. "Yes, since this summer when Mike went off on the rodeo circuit." Her gaze remained on the shenanigans of man and beast in the corral, yet every cell of her body seemed singularly aware of Quent. How odd to feel like a stranger with the person who used to tie your shoelaces, she thought. Time—it had a way of changing things.

"I had occasion to see Mike up in Denver a few weeks ago. Rodeo seems to be agreeing with him," Quent said of Cassie's older brother, giving a grin. "And he's not doing too badly with the ladies, either."

"Yes, on both counts, I suppose." She spared him a glance. "Springer's over the moon about you being transferred home and you two being able to work together." Flipping her long hair from her shoulder, she returned her attention to the corral. It was the third try, and still the man had not managed to put the hat on the furry beast. The animal wasn't pleased about the attempts, either. Quent called out good-natured advice to the young man.

"I saw your mother at the bank yesterday," Cassie said. "She's so excited about you coming home to live."

"Yes, she's pleased," Quent drawled, giving an indulgent smile. "Though I doubt she'll ever approve of my becoming a ranger."

Cassie nodded. "I can understand that." A whisper echoed within—*I can understand.*

She glanced thoughtfully to Springer, then back to Quent. Yes, she understood his mother's feelings very well, though she also knew that very few things pleased Marjean Hatfield. It was just the woman's nature. And Marjean had had her heart set on her son following his father in becoming a doctor. Quent would have never been content to spend so much of his time trapped indoors, though. Very much like her brothers, Cassie mused knowingly, very much.

Hadley moved to Quent's other side, and the two men began talking. Then Cassie heard April Sewell's voice. Glancing over, she saw the young woman sidling up close to Quent.

April Sewell, Cassie noted dryly in that instant, was a woman who was equipped with a special radar to detect any gathering of males. It was no surprise that, though this was only the second day Quent had been home, she had found him and was zeroing in on target. Maybe it was some special scent, Cassie mused, actually giving the matter halfway serious thought as she squinted in the bright sunlight, watching the buffalo elude the man in the corral and listening to April oohing and aahing.

Cassie never could understand why April discarded her brains when her eyes lit on a male of the species. Perhaps because Cassie had been born and raised in a house full of men, she had scant understanding of other females and often found her own femininity a puzzle as well as a source of conflict. She had no patience with flirting games, seldom cried and kept her emotions very well hidden, occasionally even denied them.

The man in the corral made a final shot with the hat, but the buffalo shook his furry head and blew, moving to the side, his stomping feet shaking the ground and stirring up dust.

Good-natured cheers and jeers sounded from around the corral as the young man retrieved the battered cowboy hat from the ground, then scurried out of the buffalo's way. With a call to Quent, he sailed the hat toward him. Quent caught it easily, and there was a round of clapping, hoots and whistles, urging Quent on as he flashed a confident grin and eased his lean body through the rails.

Cassie's heart fluttered apprehensively as she took in the rowdy laughter and cheers. Springer climbed to sit on the top rail, and the dust billowed softly around Quent's boots as he moved carefully into the corral, his strides easy and smooth. She wished he wouldn't do it, prayed he wouldn't get hurt.

While still in the middle of the corral, he froze for a long moment. Watching him, the beast quieted. Then with a fluid swift movement, Quent sailed the hat through the air. Seeming to catch an air current, it drifted the distance, then gently landed, catching sideways on one horn.

Right there in the middle of the ring, Quent gave a matador's bow to the applause of his audience while the buffalo behind him shook his head in fury to remove the humiliating hat. Snorting again, the animal darted forward, but with sleek, sure strides Quent reached the railing and slipped through, still casting his easy grin.

"All right, buddy," Springer called. "I'll bet ten I can get it between the animal's horns."

Cassie looked anxiously at her hulking brother, words of caution on the tip of her tongue. She choked them back, as well as the impulse to physically pull at his arm and restrain him from walking into the corral. He wouldn't appreciate such from his sister. He was a man, not a child; he didn't need correction, though Cassie vehemently thought that he did as he slowly moved toward the massive buffalo. Springer was on foot, for goodness' sake, and a buffalo could move much faster than anyone would guess.

It swept over her then, tearing at her, a feeling she hated but had come to know quite well. Fear. Not something that simply sent her adrenaline pumping, but an irrational kind that seemed to swamp her. Even though she could recognize it as irrational, she couldn't shake it.

She stood quite still, her face a blank mask. No one would ever guess how she felt; she didn't intend for them to. This fear didn't match the rest of her. She was a self-confident, practical woman who kept her head in any emergency. It was her image of herself, and also the image others had of her.

Springer sailed the hat, and everyone seemed to hold his breath. And he did it! The hat set down squarely atop the buffalo's furry head. Cassie joined in the applause, relief sweeping her. Now Springer would stop the nonsense and get out of the corral.

But the buffalo had reached his limit of humiliation. With a loud snort he charged after Springer, his hooves shaking the ground. Like a batter rushing for home plate, Springer dove for the ground and rolled beneath the bottom rail of the corral. It all happened so fast that Cassie had no time for conscious thought, only reaction. She started running toward him, intent only on making sure her younger brother was unharmed.

There seemed to be a roaring in her ears, a combination of rushing blood, yelling voices, thudding and the splintering of wood. Then wide boards were flying every which way as a massive ball of brown fur exploded just in front of Cassie. Something smacked into her thigh, and she fell to her knees, her vision a blur of lumber, hooves, dust, and Springer's blue shirt.

"Springer!" she screamed, fear and horror clawing at her as she struggled to rise. She was at his side in seconds, only vaguely aware that her right leg was having trouble bending.

With a dust-smudged face, Springer tried to sit up, giving a smile that turned quickly to a grimace. Frantically Cassie scanned his body, looking for traces of blood or torn clothing. Oddly finding none, she was unable to understand.

There were voices and movement around her. She felt surrounded by legs. And dust, so much dust. Her gaze returned to Springer's face. He was looking at her strangely, and then Quent's face shimmered before her eyes. He spoke to her. She saw his mouth moving, but couldn't hear any words.

To her immense horror, she realized she was sinking into a faint. She couldn't. She simply couldn't! *Cassie Marlow did not faint!*

Cassie's wide blue eyes were open, staring at him, but in an eerie, unseeing way. There was a rawness written on her expression that sent a cold feeling through Quent's spine.

"Cassie?" he said, uncertain that she would even hear him. Reaching quickly across Springer's legs, he grabbed her elbow to keep her from falling.

Springer cast a puzzled glance from his sister to Quent.

"She's about to faint!" Quent shot at the younger man impatiently. Springer scrambled to move as Quent reached to take Cassie with both hands. Cassie's gaze remained on his face, and he caught a flicker of recognition returning to her eyes.

"Cassie?"

She shook her head slightly. "I . . ." She blinked, seeming to bring herself back from far away. She couldn't get her breath.

"Put your head down," Quent commanded. She resisted, so he pushed her head down with his hand. The Cassie he could recognize was returning. She had never done anything anyone told her. "Cassie, come on."

She shook his hand away. "I'm okay," she insisted. "I'm okay. Springer?"

"Hey, Cass. I'm fine. Damn animal never touched me." Brushing dust from his clothes, Springer gave his charming grin and rose stiffly to his feet.

Feeling Cassie tremble, Quent swiftly stood and lifted her into his arms. She had smudges on her face, a tear in her jeans, and one of those flying boards could have hit her head. Something had obviously knocked the wind from her sails. Perhaps one of the buffalo's hooves had hit her, Quent thought.

"What are you doing?" Cassie asked sharply.

"I'm taking you over to have a look at you," Quent answered patiently as he walked in long strides to the cab of his pickup, away from the laughter and general commotion going on around them.

"I'm not an invalid. I can walk," Cassie argued, kicking her feet and pushing at his chest. "And you don't need to have a look at me."

Ah, here was the Cassie he remembered. The I-can-do-it-myself girl, equal to and better than many a man. As Quent recalled, it was what had always irritated him about her.

"Be still! You're not a feather," he ordered gruffly.

"Then put me down," she said through clenched teeth, her vivid blue eyes shooting daggers.

"You've cut your leg," he said, ignoring her protests. She hadn't noticed and stopped all her wiggling to straighten her leg and take a look.

No, she wasn't a feather, Quent thought as he reached his truck. She was firm in his arms. In nine years she'd filled out from the skinny girl she'd been at eighteen. Again he found his gaze straying to her full breasts. When he glanced at her eyes, he knew he'd been caught with his more lusty thoughts. It was annoying to find himself reddening slightly even as he smiled. Cassie had a way of looking dryly disapproving, though she said not one word.

Cassie Marlow wasn't given to jabbering or to pointing when a person made an ass of themselves. At least not with words. But that was probably what he had always *liked* about her, Quent thought as he fumbled to open the pickup door and plopped Cassie upon the seat.

He saw that her face was still exceedingly pale, and with a hand to her chin, he turned her head to have a better look, still suspecting a blow to her head. It wasn't like Cassie to faint or to become disoriented as she had. But then, he reminded himself, he'd not seen her in a long time. No doubt she'd changed.

She drew away. "What are you doing?"

"Checking to see if you'd been hit on the head. Boards and buffalo were flying all over the place." What in the hell had he done that was so awful? Quent puzzled to himself. All he'd done was try to help her. Why was she so touchy?

"I wasn't hit." She looked past him.

Glancing back, Quent followed her gaze and saw that she was looking at Springer, who was luxuriating in the attentions of April Sewell. From what Quent could see, he'd suddenly developed a few injuries needing a woman's touch.

"I think he's being cared for." Quent chuckled, turning back to lift Cassie's leg, placing her boot above his knee. She was tall and long-legged—all the Marlows were. Her pant leg below the knee was ripped, from a nail, he judged, that had also sliced a gash in her leg. The wound had bled readily enough, cleaning itself, and was already drying.

She bent her head to look at the cut, and Quent caught the scent of roses. Her hair was a rare sight—long, held by a clip at the back of her head and falling in waves to near her waist. It was the characteristic blond hair of the Marlows, but hers was tinged with red, a dead giveaway to her temperament, Quent mused inwardly. The memory came fleetingly—she used to wear it free and loose.

"Had a tetanus shot recently?" he asked.

"Recently enough," she said.

She looked up then, and Quent found himself staring into eyes as wide and blue as the western sky in winter. In them he caught a startling glimpse of the girl he'd known from childhood, mingled with the woman she had become. And he sensed danger. The same danger that had sent him traveling fast and far from his hometown nine years before.

They both seemed to look away at the same time. Quent opened the glove compartment, pulled out several tissues and surprised Cassie by beginning to wipe at her face.

"I can do it," Cassie said, averting her head. If he thought he was going to treat her like the other women he came on to, he'd find himself sadly mistaken. She hadn't missed his gaze toward April Sewell only seconds before. She knew him and his type. She'd grown up with it.

"How are you going to see where the dirt is?" Quent asked.

"You do have a mirror."

Inclining his head, he shrugged.

Bending forward, she used the large side mirror. It would have helped if she'd had a bit of water, but she wasn't about to suggest Quent wet the tissue with the melted ice in the cooler. They seemed very much alone, though the voices of the others could easily be heard. Several people had left, and the rest of them congregated over at Springer's truck, sipping beer and laughing about what had happened. Once a safe distance away from the humiliating actions of the humans, the buffalo had sensibly stopped to graze contentedly.

The gash in her leg hurt some, and Cassie could feel the spot where something had hit her thigh, otherwise she was fine.

Why did Quent continue to stand so close? And why did he continue to stare at her?

"The smart thing would have been to run away from where the buffalo wanted through, not toward it," Quent commented.

Cassie paused, but gave no reply. She didn't owe him an explanation. She simply returned to rubbing the last smudge from her cheek.

"What were you going to do? Throw yourself on Springer as a shield? Hasn't he sort of outgrown such protection?"

Her eyes flashed at the implication of his words, but she stubbornly refused to give in to a retort, hoping that her refusal to reply would annoy Quent. But to her irritation, a mellow knowing smile slipped across his face.

April Sewell joined them. "You all right, Cassie?" she asked in her sweet Southern drawl. A woman from Georgia couldn't sound more Southern than April. Her question was for Cassie, but her flirting gaze was for Quent. Quent's eyes definitely responded.

"How's Springer?" Cassie asked pointedly.

April cast her a vacant look, then said, "Oh, he's scratched some. I told him it served him right. He ought not to have been teasing the poor animal." She gave a light chuckle, again looking at Quent. Cassie felt like an intruder.

Slowly she wadded the tissues she'd used into a ball, then stuffed them into Quent's hand.

"Thanks for their use," she said, slipping from the seat to the ground, indicating she wanted to get by.

"You're welcome." He moved back a foot.

Cassie took a step, finding her leg stiff. Her shoulder brushed Quent's chest.

"You all right?" he asked quickly.

Cassie nodded. "Just stiff."

"Let me drive you home."

April frowned at Cassie.

"I can manage fine," Cassie assured Quent. She took another step. "See, good as new." She turned and walked away with quiet decorum, forcing her leg to move smoothly, though it wanted desperately to limp.

Chapter Two

By the time Cassie made it to the road, she'd worked the tendency to limp from her leg. She wasn't really angry, she told herself. Well, maybe she was—she was certainly irritated.

April Sewell really rankled Cassie, and for a moment she tried to let this go. Most women were rankled by April, and she wasn't worth the energy of anger. Quent's reaction to April shouldn't have surprised her in the least. As Cassie clearly recalled, Quent, like her brothers, had learned to appreciate females at an early age.

She shook her head, regretting that she'd made a fool of herself in front of Quent. Of course she shouldn't have run toward the bull—she just hadn't been thinking. She gave the pickup door a hard slam as she slipped into the seat. It had been the fear making her lose all sensible thought. She understood it, understood where it came from, but often couldn't do anything about it.

How like her mother she was at times, Cassie thought, unhappy with the knowledge.

Of course, since she'd rather forget it, the fearful and humiliating memory of those moments when the bull had charged Springer and she'd gone rather crazy continued to play back through her mind as she drove the short distance home. As she pulled to a stop in front of the garage, her gaze lit on a rope swing hanging from the giant elm in the yard. In a flash she pictured herself at eight or nine years of age and Quent and Mike pushing her higher and higher. Why, that swing had to be twenty years old, she realized with awe, walking slowly toward it.

It had hung there for years, forgotten, except maybe when the yard was mowed. Cassie couldn't remember the last time she'd sat in it. She did so now gingerly, testing its strength. Their hound, Cork, lumbered over to be petted, then lay down and closed his fleshy eyes. Cork wasn't given to unnecessary moves. Pushing lightly with one leg, Cassie swung back and forth, and with the wonder of memory heard again the sounds of children playing.

Cassie had three brothers: Mike, older and now living on his own; and Springer and Jesse, both younger than her. And it seemed that ever since she could remember there had been Quent. As Mike's best friend, Quent had always been there. Cassie suspected that Quent's preferring to spend most of his time at the Marlow house had something to do with Marjean Hatfield being so hard to please and keeping plastic protectors on all their furniture. Quent had teased Cassie and scolded her, helped her up into trees and down again. In every sense of the word, except biological, he'd been her brother.

Until that day at the river, that hot summer day. And their relationship had been forever changed. Pushing the swing with her toe, Cassie allowed memory full control....

She'd managed to slip away from home, and not taking time for a saddle, had ridden her horse bareback across pastures and through woods to the river. Her hair was loose, blowing behind her, adding to the feeling of freedom. The river at that moment was summer-shallow. She splashed the mare through the water, then slid down and let the reins trail in the sand as she waded, sprinkling the tepid water up on her thighs in an effort to cool off.

A voice calling out her name in the stillness startled her, and she jumped, lost her balance and fell into the murky water, wetting her shorts and part of her blouse.

A few seconds later her fright vanished when she recognized Quent standing on the riverbank, laughing. Cassie just sat there, laughing, too. Devilishly she planned to get back at him. Quent walked down to the water, and she acted as though she couldn't get up. When he took her hand to help her, she pulled him in. He hadn't expected it, or she'd never have been able to do it. She giggled and splashed him, and he splashed her. The water was milk-warm and oh-so-gritty.

Finally they dragged themselves out and walked over to sit on the bank. Cassie reclined on her elbows, and Quent did the same as a natural companionship settled over them. They were still chuckling as Quent promised revenge and Cassie dared him.

His eyes twinkled merrily as she looked at him. Then slowly the twinkling faded, his eyes growing darker. Something intimate and fiery sparked between them.

Quent's brown hair turned golden as the sunlight filtered through the leaves and played upon his head. It was the color of a bobcat, and his soft brown eyes were touched with the same gold. Cassie had never noticed before, but found it fascinating now. Gradually his gaze moved to fall heavily on her lips.

It came to her in a rush, the knowledge that she was a woman of eighteen, and he was a man of twenty-one. His wet T-shirt was plastered against his wiry frame, plainly revealing the hard muscles of his chest and stomach. Cassie very much wanted to feel his lips on hers.

In reaction to the pulsing that threaded through her body, she sucked in her breath. Mesmerized, she watched Quent's lips move to meet hers.

Then he was kissing her, softly at first. It was as if they were testing each other. Then heat flamed between them, and instinctively Cassie wrapped her arms around his neck, welcoming him with her parted lips. He pushed her back against the warm sand, his hard chest crushing her breasts.

Their kiss deepened with rising passion. Quent's hands touched her softly, exploringly, causing a strange and wonderful longing to throb within Cassie. She felt herself melting into him, absorbed by him. The wind sang high above in the branches of the tall cottonwoods—the sky was bluer, the sun brighter, the birds' calls sweeter.

In the swirling of that instant Cassie realized fully that she and Quent were no longer children, and that no male had ever made her feel such a way—so wonderfully alive, yet so wonderfully lost at the same time.

Quent broke away almost with a jerk. He looked at her for a long moment, his eyes mirroring the shock she herself felt. *How in the world had it happened?* Then more quietly the thought came to her—*what in the world had happened?* And still, as she looked at him, she felt the heat pounding in her body, the desire to be in his arms again.

Slowly Quent straightened her shirt. She just sat there looking at him, oddly unable to move. He brushed his knuckles across her cheek, stood up and pulled her up beside him.

"I'm sorry, Cass—" He broke off, looking uncertain and embarrassed, and his embarrassment made her embarrassed. She hated that he was sorry. He seemed eager to be rid of her, and she wondered what she'd done wrong.

He'd come to the house several times after that, but had definitely seemed ill at ease. That was fine for Cassie. She didn't want anything to do with Quentin Hatfield. She knew his ways too well. Yet when she'd seen him going to the movies with another girl, it had almost killed her....

She smiled now. How dreadful everything is when you're eighteen.

Two months later Quent had left for the air force. Cassie hadn't seen him since then, even though for the past two years he'd been doing ranger work in the northeastern part of the state and had come home quite a few times in the past nine years to visit his parents, Marjean and Dr. Tom Hatfield.

Now he'd come home for good, Springer had said. Cassie gave a soft sigh. He and Springer, rangers together. They'd make a fine pair. Wildlife would be safe, but the county may not.

He hadn't changed all that much, she mused. Oh, he was older: his eyes reflected a certain knowledge, his movements were smooth and fluid, and the cockiness of youth was replaced by the quiet confidence of a man. But he still had that edge about him. A rounder, a rogue. And Cassie knew that type of man very well. They had colored her world all of her life.

She could easily see why Quent had become a ranger—it suited him. Just as it did Springer, and as it had her father. Officially rangers were under the Wildlife Division of the state government. They worked in all areas of wildlife management, from hunting control to tagging deer to setting up refuge areas. It was a job close to nature and the earth, requiring a man to spend hours outside, many of them alone. It gave a man freedom, room to move, with no one to constantly look over his shoulder, no walls hemming him in.

But rangers also had the full powers of all law officers. And along with the power came the danger. A ranger's work could be eight times more dangerous than a police officer's in the city because he generally worked alone, in isolated areas. The majority of the people he dealt with had guns and used them every day—not only the legal hunters and the poachers, but also the farmers and ranchers who carried rifles in their trucks when they tended their land. It was a way of life.

It was the freedom, the oneness with nature and the edge of danger that made the job and made the men who did the job. They were a special breed, a romantic, charming, untamed breed.

But Cassie didn't find them all that charming. After all, she was the woman behind the men, so to speak, and knew the harder, factual edge to it all. She was intimately familiar with their rowdy ways, with the long hours and even days when the men would be gone, of calls in the night—and remembered one horrifying night in particular when she'd received the call telling her their father wouldn't be coming home again.

She'd made up her mind long ago, when she was very young and her mother was still alive—sometime during the hours she'd joined her mother in watching through the window for her father to come home—that she would never get involved with a man anywhat remotely resembling the men of her family. Her resolve had hardened into granite as she'd listened to the hard lumps of clay fall upon her father's casket. He'd been shot on duty. That was the harder, factual side of being a ranger.

She wanted a man who would be home every night by six o'clock, Cassie thought emphatically, and weekends. A man who enjoyed sitting by the fire, reading, watching television, and who would regard her as more than some feminine fluff to keep his house and warm his bed.

All the women out there were welcome to one Quentin Hatfield.

With a hard push Cassie swung herself into the air. The tree limb above groaned, but not dangerously so. She pumped higher, flying back and forth in the air. Then, relaxing, she allowed the natural pendulum of the swing to gently slow.

The next instant the swing jerked to one side. There was no time to move before the swing broke, and her buttocks met the hard ground as one side of the rope fell across her head.

She sat there, thinking—that this was the reality of life, and destined to become one of those sour memories. To make matters worse, little brother Jesse picked that minut to roar into the driveway on his three-wheeler. He st laughing, of course.

"Need a diet, Cassie?" he teased, removing his helmet and flopping his blond hair from his forehead. "When's dinner? I'm starved."

Her cue, of course, Cassie thought with a small grin as she rose to her feet. Since she'd been able to reach the water faucets at the sink, she'd gradually taken over the duties of keeping the home. Her mother had never been strong, or inclined to cooking and cleaning. She had lived much of her life worrying herself sick over her husband, and spending her days more in dreams than reality. She'd died when Cassie was thirteen, when Jesse was still in diapers, and from then on Cassie had been mother to all the Marlow boys, and even to her father until his death. It was Cassie's nature.

"You do that on the swing?" Jesse asked, nodding to her torn pant leg.

"No—earlier." Cassie shook her head. "What do you want to eat?"

"Macaroni and cheese," Jesse replied.

"You got it," Cassie said with a grin.

It was a Sunday that had dawned rainy and had produced the kind of fall day that made a person grateful for hot coffee and a dry home.

Cassie sat at the kitchen table with bills, receipts and ledgers spread out in front of her. She was struggling with the store accounts. Struggling was an apt word, she thought, then gave a wry inward smile. Marlow Feed and Grain was family-owned, but Cassie-run. She wasn't sure how it had all evolved, except that somewhere in history, before her time, the business had more or less been left to the women of the family.

Brushing stray hairs from her forehead, she gave a small sigh of ____ tion. More accounts than ever before were ____ 'mes were hard; farmers and ranchers were ____ bills, even to keep their land. The store ____ o, but Cassie couldn't find it in her heart ____ owed. Some of these people she'd known ____ school and church with them.

Besides, she and her brothers were set nicely and could afford to carry the store, at least for a while. Their house and land were free of debt. And though at the moment the store was losing money, they had Springer's income, an annuity from their father for Jesse, and enough land to run a few head of cattle and raise vegetables for the family table.

The drone of the television from the living room filtered through the swinging door. Jesse was watching motorcycle racing. Every now and again he added his own sound effects—he'd done this as a child, still did it now in his teens.

The figures on the papers seemed to blur. Tossing aside the pencil, Cassie rubbed her eyes, then looked to the window. It reflected her image dotted with rain drops. Though it was only six o'clock in the evening, it was dark already.

Crossing the room, Cassie bent to stroke Cork's back. "Aren't you glad I'm a softy," she murmured. The hound opened his fleshy eyes and thumped his tail slowly in response, but that was all.

The kitchen door burst inward as Springer entered, leaving the door swinging behind him.

"Where's a clean pair of socks, Cassie?" he bellowed in his deep voice. "And why do my best boots have mud all over them?" A big bear of a man, he was often as helpless as a babe, Cassie thought, looking at him. All three of her brothers were the same in this respect.

"Talk to Jesse about your boots," she said calmly. "And the socks can't be washed if you don't ever put them in the dirty clothes bin." She walked to the back of the kitchen, stepped through the laundry room door and returned with a clean pair of socks.

Grunting in mild annoyance, Springer sat and pulled them on. Cassie poured two cups of coffee and set one in front of him.

"Your boots aren't the only thing you need to talk to Jesse about," she said, almost nervously. She'd never talked to Springer about the facts of life, but now she was going to have to, in connection with Jesse.

"What's he been up to now?" Springer asked, buffing a brush across his boot.

"I found a note in his pants pocket. I couldn't believe what a girl would write to him." Cassie recalled the note with a mixture of amazement and embarrassment. It had seemed to burn her hands just to hold it.

"So even the youngest of us has the gift with women, huh?" Springer gave a pleased grin.

"Springer, this is serious," Cassie said sternly. "Sex is...is...well, it's not a game. Especially at fifteen. You have to talk to him."

Springer kept his eyes on his boots. "Let it go, Cassie. You'll hurt his pride. He's been raised a certain way. It's up to him now."

"He's only fifteen—that's hardly a man," she countered stubbornly. "You need to caution him."

"You do it—you're best at that sort of thing, anyway," Springer said, hedging.

Cassie had spoiled her brothers; she knew it. They leaned on her, shying away from as much responsibility as possible. And it was mostly her fault for allowing them to do it. She was the rock of the family, the strong, practical one who kept order at home, who kept order at the store, who kept order in all their lives. She was supposed to have all the answers, and they never realized she often had a great many questions, too.

"It should be you who talks to him." Her tone dropped. "You're a man—and his brother."

Springer pulled on his boots. "Okay, but not tonight." He flashed his charming grin. "Got a date."

With a small sigh of exasperation, she let the subject drop.

Springer took his slicker from the coat rack near the door. "Oh, I almost forgot. I've invited a few guys—" He stopped, looking sheepish. "Well, quite a few people over Friday night—a get-together of some of the old gang to celebrate Quent's coming home. And for Quent to meet some of the new people around here. Better get some soft drinks, beer, and stuff."

"Springer," Cassie moaned in disgust, "did you ever once think of asking me?"

"I live here, too."

"Yes, but it's me you want to handle your party," Cassie pointed out. She'd do it. He knew she would. She just wished he wouldn't take her for granted.

"That's because you're so good at it." Giving a devilish grin, he tugged at her ponytail. "Besides, Quent's your friend, too."

Cassie gave him a mildly reproachful look for good measure.

Springer slipped into his slicker. "Did I tell you Quent brought a helicopter home with him?" he said. "His own damn chopper." His voice echoed with wonder.

"He did?" Cassie asked in mild surprise. Springer must have told her about his and Quent's every move in the past week. How could he have missed this bit of information? There were only three rangers in the state who flew. They had planes. "It ought to come in handy for you guys," Cassie added.

"Damn straight," Springer said. "We'll be able to cover a lot more territory when we have to."

"Great. Now that Quent's here with his helicopter, you two can ride and fly the range together." Even as dry humor laced her voice, she reached up and fastened the top button of his slicker and gave his chest a gentle pat. "I just hope you both can manage to stay out of trouble."

"Aw, Cass, what fun would that be?" Springer's eyes twinkled. He glanced at the books on the table. "You ought to leave that mess and come with me tonight. April's having a few people out to her ranch." At her disapproving look, Springer held up his hands. "I'll be the soul of propriety, I promise, Sis. Come on—Quent'll be there."

Cassie shook her head.

"Come on," Springer coaxed. "All work and no play makes Cassie a dull girl. Don't you want to see Quent? All the other females do. We couldn't even have a quiet beer together last night for all the women who kept interrupting us."

"I'm hardly like all the females. I've known Quent since I was able to share your jeans and we were all watching cartoons together."

Springer looked at her for a long moment. "I get your point, Cassie," he said, his voice unusually quiet. "But maybe you better look in the mirror. You're hardly that little girl anymore." Bending, he brushed a light kiss across her forehead. "I won't be past midnight."

What a thing to say, Cassie thought as she watched Springer's truck splash through the drive and disappear down the road. She knew she wasn't a little girl anymore. Sometimes she felt she never had been a little girl: from the time she could remember she'd been taking care of the house, of the family.

She gave a soft sigh. At least Springer wasn't going off on duty in this weather, she thought with mild relief. She wouldn't be plagued with worry this night. She almost wished she'd gone with him. It probably would be fun.... She pictured Quent in her mind. So all the women were delighted he was home, huh? Well, that came as no surprise at all.

This kind of ridiculous thinking was getting her nowhere, Cassie told herself firmly and returned to the store ledgers. But she couldn't keep her mind on them. When the telephone rang, interrupting her, she was glad. It was Anita Reid.

"I know it's rotten outside," Anita told her, "but do you suppose you could come over for a while? Perry was called out, and I feel a little funny. I'd just rather not be alone." Anita's husband Perry worked for an oil company and often had to be away working on rigs in outlying areas.

"What do you mean 'a little funny?'" Cassie asked quickly. Anita was eight months pregnant with her first child. "Have you called Dr. Tom?"

"Just a little funny. The baby's been kicking up a storm for two hours. And I'm not going to call Dr. Tom yet," she said emphatically. "I'm not due for two more weeks, and I can't call Dr. Tom again, Cassie," Anita fairly wailed. "I've had three false alarms already. I can't bear to do it again."

"I'll be over in a few minutes," Cassie said, laughter lacing her voice.

"I'm sorry—" Anita began, but Cassie cut her off.

"It's okay. I'd rather be over there with you than here doing these blasted store accounts."

"Oh, Cassie," Anita asked meekly, "do you have any ice cream?"

"Mint chocolate-chip," she offered, chuckling.

"That'll do—thanks a million."

Slipping into her slicker, Cassie pulled a half gallon container of ice cream from the freezer. "I'm going over to Anita's," she told Jesse in the living room.

His long frame was stretched belly-down on the couch, and his blond hair waved across his forehead and into his eyes. Two empty soda cans and a bag of chips lay nearby on the floor. Just when she was sure she'd spoken to a log and had turned to leave, Jesse broke his attention from the television.

"Think you ought to with all this rain, Sis?"

His concern touched her, and she ruffled his hair. "Anita's alone right now—I'll be okay."

Jesse grabbed her hand. "Want me to go with you?"

"No, I may end up staying all night if Perry can't get back. I don't want to leave Anita alone." She looked stern. "You stay out of Springer's beer."

"Aw, Cassie, I'm old enough to have a beer if I feel like it," Jesse argued.

"Fifteen is not old enough. And you better stay home, too. I'll call from Anita's."

Gusty wind blew drops of water at her as Cassie walked beneath the covered breezeway to the garage. Rain thudded against the pickup roof and poured across the windshield as she backed her truck from the building. Though the roads were bound to be slick, she wasn't worried. Her pickup had four-wheel drive, and she knew the roads well. The sandy-clay road in front of their house ran with water, but the truck managed it easily, and in minutes Cassie pulled onto the blacktopped state highway, heading for Doyle City, her mind turning sharply to Anita.

In just over five minutes she pulled into the short drive beside Anita's small bungalow. Covering her head with the hood of her slicker, she ran through the rain, which seemed to have eased, pounded on the door, then entered.

"Anita?" she called, looking around. The living room was empty. Anita wasn't in the kitchen, either. Putting the ice cream in the freezer, Cassie returned to the living room at the same time that Anita appeared from the hallway. Anita's face looked ashen in the palely lit room. "Are you all right?" Cassie asked quickly.

"I'm not sure," Anita said slowly. "I think I may have started with contractions."

"Oh, Lord," Cassie breathed. "Are you sure?"

Anita's eyes widened. "Of course not—I've never done this before. And it certainly doesn't seem like what I've read in the books."

Cassie reached for the telephone. "I'm calling Dr. Tom."

Quent hung up the phone, mild disappointment tugging at him. He'd called the Marlows to speak to Springer. It put him off balance when Jesse's voice came over the line instead of Cassie's. Springer had left, and Cassie had gone to a friend's, Jessie had told him.

Well, he asked himself, what did he expect? He wasn't sure. He guessed he'd halfway hoped to hear Cassie's voice. He'd even toyed with the idea of asking her to join them tonight, but instinct told him that wasn't her style. Cassie never had been one much for large, noisy groups. And instinct also told him she probably wasn't much for April Sewell, either.

He raked a hand through his thick hair, still wet from a shower. He didn't really want to go over to April's now. The main reason he'd agreed to go was his need to have a few minutes' peace from his mother, he thought guiltily. His mother was a loving woman, but definitely hard to please. And she hovered over him, wanting to grant the desires of her only child before he even knew what they were, to the point that Quent felt suffocated.

But now he had the house to himself for a few hours. His father had been called out on an emergency, and his mother had gone along to help. He'd kind of like to put up his feet and watch television.

The shrill ringing of the wall telephone near his ear startled him. "Yes," Quent answered.

"I . . . Quent?"

He recognized Cassie's voice. "Yes . . . I live here, remember?" he teased, unaccountably pleased at hearing her voice. His mind immediately pictured her face, pale skin, full pink lips.

"Yes, of course." He caught the agitation in her voice. "I just thought—Springer said you were meeting him and some others over at April's tonight."

"I haven't gotten there yet," Quent answered. "What's up?"

"I need to speak to your father," she said, and he sensed something was wrong.

"He's out—emergency over at the Crawford place. Something wrong? Where are you? At home?"

"No, I'm in town. At a friend's." Cassie sounded ruffled. "Do you know when Dr. Tom will be back?"

"No," Quent said. "He may have to go in to the hospital. Crawford put an ax in his foot. What is it, Cassie?" he asked for the third time.

There was a pause before she answered. "Anita Reid—she used to be Anita Johnson, married Perry Reid," she explained. Quent thought quickly, placing the names with faces. "She's pregnant," Cassie continued, "and we think her contractions have started, but the baby's not due for another two weeks, and she's had several false labors before."

"Have you tried timing the contractions?" Quent asked, his mind calculating the time needed to get to the hospital as he wiggled into a shirt with his free hand.

"No." Cassie's voice faded, and he heard her talking to someone in the background. "I think I'll drive her on over to the hospital. I'd rather be safe. Will you see if you can reach your father out at the Crawfords and tell him?"

"Yes," Quent answered. "And you sit tight, Cassie. I'll come over and drive you two to the hospital. Where's she live?"

"That's okay, Quent. I'm perfectly capable of driving." Cassie's tone was that of a patient elder's to a child. "I've driven these roads since I was able to see over the steering wheel."

Quent matched her tone. "I know you're capable, Cass. But you two women don't need to be out in this weather alone. Now, where's she live?"

Cassie sighed. "Up the hill from your place, end of the street and two blocks over."

"Be there in a minute," Quent quipped, then hung up before she could possibly think of arguing further.

He looked up the number of the Crawfords, called, and learned that his father and mother and the elder Crawford had just left for the hospital minutes before. Quent then called the hospital to leave a message for his father.

Pushing his Stetson low on his forehead against the misty rain, he left the house for his truck. At least the drenching rain had slowed. It crossed his mind that he'd heard his father say that babies tended to be born when the barometer dropped. It could very well be that Anita Reid was ready to deliver, two weeks early or not.

He found the Reid house easily. His headlights shone brightly upon a midnight-blue pickup that he figured belonged to Cassie.

The front door was ajar. Tapping his knuckles lightly, Quent pushed at the door and entered. The dim light of a nearby lamp shimmered golden on the long ponytail trailing down Cassie's back. She knelt on the floor in front of

Anita, who sat in a chair. Quent saw at once that Anita was definitely having a contraction. He heard Cassie softly coaxing her to breathe.

Chapter Three

In the minutes since Cassie had called the Hatfield home, Anita had had one mild contraction and now this harder one. Cassie insisted that Anita call Perry's work and leave a message for them to locate him. She was convinced this was no false alarm, and the quicker they got to the hospital, the better she'd feel.

She looked to Quent with relief when he entered, sensing calm strength in his easy smile.

"Hello, ladies. How's it going?" he said in his mellow voice, though Cassie noticed his eyes went sharply from herself to Anita.

"Hello, Quent," Anita said. "Nice way to see you again. Dr. Tom told me you'd come home."

Slowly, finding her legs stiff, Cassie straightened. "It appears the contractions have truly started," she told Quent as she bent to help Anita, who was trying to rise, her rotund abdomen a definite hindrance. Stepping to them quickly, Quent assisted with a strong arm around Anita's shoulders.

"Did you get Dr. Tom?" Anita asked anxiously.

Cassie, too, looked expectantly at Quent, hoping that Dr. Tom was on his way. Her heart constricted when he shook his head.

"He and Mom had already left for the hospital with Crawford," Quent said. "I called over there and left a message—told them we were on our way. How close are the contractions?"

"This was the first strong one," Cassie told him. "She had a soft one about the time I was talking to you."

"The baby's been kicking for hours," Anita said with agitation in her voice. "I could have been having mild contractions then." She gave Cassie an anxious glance. "I just don't know. I mean, nothing seems to feel like what it said in all those books I've read." She gently tapped her foot. "Oh, for all I know, this could be another false alarm."

"Let's just not take a chance," Cassie said calmly, putting an arm around Anita's shoulders. "You get your coat. I'll get your bag, and we'll drive over to the hospital, and let them decide exactly what's going on."

Anita nodded reluctantly, frowning. "I wish Perry were here. We had it all planned. We went to all those child-birth classes and everything."

"It'll be all right, Anita," Cassie said softly. "I know I'm not Perry, but I'll do my best to fill in."

"Thanks, Cass." Anita's eyes shone with tears. "I'll be with you in a minute," she said and rather waddled toward the bathroom.

"Couldn't you get a hold of Perry?" Quent asked.

"He's out in the field. We left a message. They'll get him as soon as they can." She looked up into Quent's eyes, which were now a soft brown, feeling the worry suddenly break over and engulf her.

"Hey," Quent said, giving his slow smile. "Babies are born every day."

It seemed only natural to let him put his comforting arms around her and to lean against his chest, to lean against his strength, as well. She'd remained calm and strong for Anita, but the plain fact was that she felt far from certain.

Suddenly self-conscious, she pushed herself away from Quent. She never cared to have someone see her other than calmly capable. It was silly, leaning on him.

"I'll get Anita's things," she said quickly, not looking again into his face.

She located the bag her friend had packed and had ready for over a month, and as a precaution she pulled two cotton thermal blankets from the hall closet. They could be needed to make Anita more comfortable on the drive to the hospital.

Quent stood waiting very quietly in the living room. He reached to take Anita's bag and the blankets from her hands. "I'll drive," he said firmly. "You check on Anita while I put these in the truck."

Cassie watched his quiet strides with relief, grateful that he was with them, but a bit irritated, as well. She wasn't used to someone arranging things for her. She was usually the one everyone else turned to and leaned on. Well, it was a blessing he was with them, she thought. That left her free to attend to Anita while he drove.

Everything was under control, she told herself firmly. Anita was doing fine. In thirty minutes they'd be at the hospital. Why, Dr. Tom was already there. Everything was going smoothly.

Until she found Anita clinging to the bathroom sink.

"The pain—it's harder, Cassie." Anita's eyes were saucer-round.

Oh, Lord, Cassie thought, glancing at her watch. It had been six minutes since the last one. Surely labor wasn't supposed to progress like this!

Aloud, forcing her voice to remain even, she said, "Okay. Don't panic, Anita. You're supposed to have contractions. Remember—they taught you in that class to call them contractions, not pains."

"They're pains!" Anita yelled as she clung to the sink while the contractions swept her abdomen.

"Okay—they're pains," Cassie agreed soothingly. "Now breathe—that's it, honey. Good. Good...you're doing fine," she coaxed, relieved to see the terror subside from Anita's eyes as the contractions ended. She checked her watch, frantically searching her memory for someone in town who had experience with this sort of thing. She couldn't think of a soul, and the hospital was still thirty minutes away—likely forty on a night like this.

Quent appeared at Cassie's shoulder. "What's happening?"

"Another contraction, a harder one." She cast him a worried glance. "It's only been six minutes since the last one. What do you think?"

"It's okay yet," Quent said, putting a hand on her shoulder. "But let's get going."

Anita had to gather her shampoo, creams and makeup. And she insisted that Cassie scurry around to let the cat in and that she unplug all the electrical cords. They were at the front door, helping Anita into her coat when she went into another contraction. It had barely been four minutes since the last one. Holding Anita's hand, Cassie looked anxiously at Quent.

"We'll have to use the chopper," he said, putting his arms around Anita's shoulders. "Come on, Anita." He lifted her easily.

"The chopper?" Cassie said, and Anita's voice echoed behind hers.

Quent nodded, whisking Anita through the door. "I've got it setting over behind the police station. We can get there in a third of the time it would take to drive."

"On a night like this?" Cassie countered as she ran behind him to the truck, ducking her head against the misty rain. It was a fool idea. Couldn't he see the rain and wind? She jumped into the passenger side of the truck beside Anita. "Quent?"

"I can handle it, Cassie," he said starting the engine. "Besides, it's only drizzling now."

"It's a crazy idea." Cassie adjusted one of the blankets around Anita. "We'd be better off in the truck than flying around up there in the dark and the rain. We'll be at the hospital in thirty minutes—and on the ground.''

"In the chopper, we'll be there in ten," Quent said, backing up quickly. "Look, I know what I'm doing. I've flown at night—in the rain—a hundred times."

"Can I get a word in here since I'm the main one involved?" Anita broke in. Her face was exceedingly pale, and Cassie realized she was close to tears. "I want to have my baby at the hospital. I'm afraid. Yesterday when I saw Dr. Tom, he said the baby hadn't turned. He said it could be breech."

"He said this yesterday?" Cassie asked quickly.

Anita nodded.

"You've not felt it turn or anything?" Quent asked sharply.

Anita shook her head. "How would I know? I don't know what it feels like—oh..." Her eyes widened with pain as another contraction started.

Cassie's heart constricted. It had been less than four minutes since the last one, she was sure. She took Anita's hand, and her friend squeezed it hard. Cassie felt panic rising in her throat as Anita bent slightly.

"Breathe, honey," she whispered, wishing she could take the pain from Anita and feeling so damn helpless it made her angry. She glanced to Quent with silent agreement for his plan. There was little choice. Anita had to get to the hospital, and soon.

The rain had turned to a fine mist, the wind slowing to a breeze. The police station parking lot glimmered beneath the light of a tall pole lamp. Fairly snatching Anita from the seat of the truck, Quent carried her to the waiting helicopter. Cassie ran along behind, bearing the suitcase and blankets. She heard a man call from the station doors but didn't take time to answer him.

Her first look at the helicopter did little to reassure her. Partially white, partially some color that looked green, and spotted with primer, it looked to have been through several wars and back again. But holding her opinion, as well as stilling her tremors, she jumped into the space between the front seats and the narrow bench-type seat in the back upon which Quent laid Anita. Crouching there, she held Anita's hand, counting seconds because it was too dim to see her watch. Her insides were crying out for Quent to hurry, though she knew he already was.

Quent jumped into the front seat, tossed his hat aside and began to flip switches. Two small lights came on, illuminating the back area with a silver glow. Taking a quick glance around, Cassie thought the interior looked as worn and doubtful as the exterior. There seemed to be a thousand knobs, switches and tiny indicator lights in front of Quent. Well, at least a hundred, she amended. The engine coughed, and coughed again. *Would it even start?* On the third cough the engine caught, the machine vibrating as the blade above made a swooping sound, faster and faster.

Quent shot Cassie a grin. "Be there in less than ten minutes, ladies," he called gallantly, raising his voice above the engine noise.

He's in his element, Cassie thought wryly, but she took strength from his self-assured manner.

In seconds the machine was lifting off the ground into the enveloping black night sky. Cassie was too busy dealing with Anita and another contraction to think about being worried. Greedily she harbored the comforting thought that they would set down in the hospital parking lot in only minutes.

Anita clutched her hand, and Cassie wished she could breathe for her friend. She could see that Anita was becoming more and more frightened and gradually losing strength.

Then Anita began to cry. "Cassie—oh, my God, Cassie—I think the baby's coming!"

"Okay, Anita...just breathe. Pant, honey. Don't push." Cassie forced assurance into her voice. "We're going to be there in just a very few minutes now."

Anita tried; she really tried. Watching her struggling with the inborn instincts of her body, Cassie found herself pant-ing and blowing, wanting so much to help her friend. But Anita's body could not be fooled. The baby was ready.

"Quent!" Cassie called above the roar of the engine. *"For God's sake, set this thing down and help me!"*

Immediately she heard the change in the engine noise, and her stomach rose as the machine descended.

Striving to remain calm, she helped Anita prepare for a very determined baby, her insides quivering with terror. She didn't know about Quent, but for herself, this wasn't an everyday occurrence. Oh, she'd watched kittens and puppies being born and had assisted in several calvings and with one colt. That hardly qualified her as an expert in this human situation.

But fear wasn't going to help anyone, she told herself firmly. So she prayed, silently *Please don't let this baby be breech.* At the same time she wondered how she'd managed to get herself into a situation like this.

The instant the chopper touched the ground, Quent cut the engines. Light. They needed more light, he thought quickly and switched on all the inner lights he could. It would do.

Okay, buddy, he told himself as he wormed his way between the seats. Here it is. Of the three people in the plane, he guessed he knew the most about delivering a baby. And that wasn't saying much. He'd soaked up some information just by being around his father, and he'd undergone training at a special emergency school. Once he'd even assisted a paramedic in delivering a baby. None of that made him an expert, but he guessed it would have to do.

"Okay, Cassie," Quent said, his heart pounding. "Get up there at Anita's shoulders and help support her." Anita was weakening from the continuing hard contractions. Cassie's face showed strain, but she remained calm.

Cassie nodded, moving quickly. Quent wormed himself around her to Anita's feet. Anita began to lose self-control and moaned, then a scream escaped her.

"Hey, Anita." He raised his voice. "This baby's coming, honey. Headfirst, just like he's supposed to." Thank

God, he echoed to himself. Anita was getting tired, Quent saw, and that was the danger. Cassie was holding her, trying to be her strength. "Just a bit more," he whispered.

The adrenaline pounded within him when he was able to hold the tiny infant by the shoulders and guide it into the world.

"It's a boy." His voice cracked as he looked at the small wriggling miracle he held in his hands.

Cassie produced a clean folded blanket. "Here, Quent. We must keep him warm," she said, as practical as ever.

Gently Quent laid the squirming child into the soft folds of the blanket, then raised his gaze to Cassie. Her eyes shimmered, and for just an instant they shared the magic exuberance of the moment. Anita pushed forward to see, and both Quent and Cassie held the baby to her, proudly, as if they'd been the ones responsible for his life.

"Under the seat, there to the side," Quent said, inclining his head. "Get that first aid box."

With shaking hands Quent used gauze and a sterile razor blade from the box to tie and cut the umbilical cord. Elation swelled within him as he watched the tiny wriggling infant. Cassie crooned softly to the child.

"But he's not crying," Anita whispered worriedly.

About that time, the infant let out a small mewl. Then his cry came louder—a resounding mewl. Quent thought he'd never heard anything so wonderful in all his life.

He felt as if he were observing from a great distance the women and the baby and even himself. The dark, misty night enfolded them as a velvet blanket. The world was a miracle, a good and wonderful miracle at that moment.

His eyes rested on Cassie's warm blond hair as she bent toward Anita, settling the baby in his mother's arms. He felt sort of dazed. He'd delivered a baby, he thought. *He'd actually just touched a brand new human being.*

Cassie raised her eyes to his, and he recognized the same emotions within her. They held each other's gaze, sharing the wonder, the joy, and something else, too, though Quent wasn't exactly sure what. For a curious instant Cassie's image blurred before his eyes to become as she had been that day, that hot summer day so long ago, her long hair wavy against her cheeks and touching her breasts, her eyes reflecting the color of the sky.

He blinked, clearing the image and coming back to the moment. Tears flowed down Cassie's cheeks, and the next instant she slumped against his chest. He felt her body shuddering with sobs; her tears wet his shirt. The baby let out a true howl.

"I think we'd better get this mother and son to the hospital," Quent said, self-consciously swallowing the lump in his throat, but unable to stop grinning. He gripped Cassie's hand in his own. She looked up at him, and Quent thought he'd burst inside from the look of female adoration she shot him. Why, he'd delivered a baby. He was a hero.

Cassie stood beside Quent and looked through the nursery window. She'd called Jesse and told him what had happened. Anita was finally relaxing in her room, and Perry should be arriving any moment. Little Perry "Q.C." Reid, as Anita was calling him, slept peacefully. Cassie felt such a feeling of protectiveness for him. She critically observed the nurse as she picked him up and adjusted his blanket.

Dr. Tom stepped into the nursery and spoke to the nurse. He waved to them, mouthing to Quent to go on home. Marjean had returned with the Crawfords.

Quent shifted beside her. He was frowning.

"What is it?" Cassie asked at last.

"The kid's too wrapped up," he stated testily. "He needs room to kick and squirm."

Cassie gazed back at little Perry. "He looks quite content to me. Babies like to have that blanket wrapped tight like that. Gives them a feeling of security."

Quent gave a disgusted snort. "Looks like a mummy. He'd do a lot better if he had room to move."

"What's wrong with the way he's doing?" she asked, mystified, peering closer, trying to find what she was missing.

"Well, he kicked around in Anita's stomach, didn't he? Sure indication he wanted out—for more room. He's trussed up there like Sunday's roast."

"He's sleeping peacefully," Cassie said, believing that proved her point.

Quent looked at her sharply but said nothing else.

A smile tugged at her lips. Quent was as protective as she, she thought, and he had a right.

He stood very near her; she was conscious of the sleeve of his jacket touching hers. Tonight was the first time Cassie could ever remember leaning on someone the way she had on Quent. It made her feel...funny, she thought. Her pride suffered a bit as she admitted it, but she didn't know what she and Anita would have done without him. Thank God she hadn't had to go through it all alone. She should tell him, her conscience prodded.

"Thank you, Quent," she managed.

He looked puzzled.

"For tonight. I don't know what we would have done without you."

His smile spread characteristically slowly beneath his mustache. "Glad I was around. You did all right, yourself, Cass. I guess that's one way you're the same—you're never ruffled easily." His eyes held a searching look, reminding Cassie of the day she'd gone quite hysterical with Springer's antics at the Smith ranch. Thank heavens Quent couldn't know what had gone on inside her.

Cassie chuckled. "No, I guess I don't—it comes from living with my three brothers." Quent chuckled, too. Together they turned from the nursery window and began walking slowly down the hall.

A few feet down against the wall was a coffee machine. Quent stopped, raising a questioning eyebrow to Cassie as he dug in his pocket for change.

"Yes, please," she said. She was suddenly tired, but content within her heart. She'd seen a brand new life come into the world. She felt as if she'd seen some sort of miracle. She looked at Quent, her gaze moving to his hands.

Those same hands that now reached for a small coffee cup had less than an hour ago gently eased a tiny boy into this world.

His eyes met hers as he handed her the steaming cup, and she knew he was experiencing the same curious exhilaration.

"It was such a miracle," she said with a slight shake of her head, seeing in memory the tiny life squiggling upon the blanket, gasping for air.

Taking a sip of coffee, Quent nodded in agreement. "We humans are pretty hardy specimens," he said.

"Have you done it before—delivered a baby?"

"Not alone," he said, giving a shake of his head. "I did have a smattering of training in it, and I helped a paramedic once. I think most of the time babies pretty well deliver themselves."

Cassie laughed. "It seemed so tonight. And he was definitely determined."

Quent smiled. Propping himself against the corridor wall, he closed his eyes. Strands of straight brown hair fell across his forehead, and fatigue etched the corners of his mouth. Cassie's gaze settled lightly on his shoulders, and she found herself thinking how strong he was. Strength fairly emanated from him, a quiet kind. And, Cassie realized, his quiet strength had helped carry her through the events of the evening. Several times she'd been so scared, so very scared for Anita and the baby.

Her gaze returned to his face to find that his soft bobcat eyes were open, staring at her. She didn't want to, but it happened, anyway—his eyes seemed to gather her to him. They darkened and searched hers, asking some sort of puzzling question. Slowly he leaned toward her. The breath caught in her throat as she naturally raised her lips, drawn by the magnetic warmth in those wide golden-brown eyes.

His lips touched hers softly, his mustache tickling her. The magnetic charge grew sharper.

As she would from fire, Cassie quickly drew back. Quent looked startled, bewildered.

"We'd better be getting home," she said.

She was enjoying the ride, Quent saw as he glanced at Cassie. She turned her face toward him, and the greenish lights from the instrument panel sparkled in her eyes. Though he couldn't tell, he imagined her full lips moist and deep pink, as they'd looked in the hospital corridor minutes before.

He puzzled over that moment. She'd acted practically like he'd slapped her, and until this moment she wouldn't meet his eyes. Apparently she hadn't wanted him to kiss her, he thought heavily. Hell, he didn't even know what had prompted him. It was a fool notion.

But surely he wasn't mistaken in thinking that she'd raised her lips to his.

"Like it?" he called to her, referring to the flight, knowing the answer but feeling a twinge of pleasure all the same when she nodded, confirming it. Cassie was a rare woman, he thought. He couldn't ever remember her being scared of anything. Once he and Mike had tried to scare her with a snake in her school lunch box. She's just pulled it out and let it go in the bushes, then scolded them for being unkind to living animals. Spoiled all their fun, he thought as a grin escaped him.

"What is it?" she asked, catching the grin.

"Memories," he answered. "Do you remember the time Mike put a snake in your lunch box?"

"That, and more." She laughed out loud then.

He shot her a glance, thinking how inviting her face looked in the dimness. "Guess you did a lot of cleaning up after us."

"Yes, guess so." Softly spoken, her words were barely audible. Quent picked up on her fatigue.

A warmness flowed between them. Quent sensed her smile more than saw it, but then he felt her pulling away. Physically she didn't move, only turned her face and looked out into the night sky. He couldn't imagine what she saw; there was only darkness.

He'd hardly set the chopper down when she unbuckled the seat belt, opened the door and dropped to the ground. The drive to her truck at Anita's was quiet.

"Thanks again," she said as he pulled to a stop.

"It's okay." He wished she'd quit thanking him. It made him feel like some stranger.

He watched her drive away, thinking: *Cassie Marlow was no one's little sister any longer.* The thought came full and hard, and he remembered the feel of her womanly body as he'd carried her that day a week ago when she'd hurt her leg.

Sprinkles of rain began to fall again, softly covering the windshield as he drove home through the quiet streets.

Perhaps, he thought, he'd come home to more than just a section of the country he knew and loved, to more than just his family and old friends. Perhaps he'd come home to the only woman who could make him remember one single kiss for nine years.

The smell of sizzling sausage and brewed coffee filled the house before Cassie made it downstairs the following morning. She had dragged herself from bed but refused to hurry.

Lettie, their housekeeper, was at the stove. Jesse had already left with a friend for school, and Springer was just finishing a second cup of coffee.

"Hello, Dr. Cassie," Springer greeted her. "Heard you had quite a night."

"Tell us all about it," Lettie said, her eyes bright with curiosity as she set a plate of eggs and a cup of coffee before Cassie.

Savoring the coffee, Cassie related the previous night's events. Told in the bright light of morning, the whole story seemed overly melodramatic. Lettie gave several oh-my's, and Springer chuckled at the thought of Quent's being caught in the situation. After curiosity was satisfied, it was back to the everyday: the washer had broken down first thing, Lettie informed her; and Springer announced he was joining a partner over in Grady County for the day. They'd had reports of illegal hunting.

"Think I'll stop by and see that little Perry at the hospital on my way," Springer said. He looked as dashing as ever, his tan-and-green ranger uniform made even more impressive by his tall, muscular frame. Cassie's gaze fell heavily on the gun strapped at his hip. "Think he and Anita will still be there?" he asked.

Cassie nodded. "But they should be able to come home this afternoon." Forcing her eyes from the gun, she sent him a parting smile. Would she ever get used to the sight of that gun? she wondered, strangely finding herself picturing Quent in the same uniform.

She sat eating her breakfast and enjoying three cups of coffee, needing the caffeine to boost her energy. When she found herself wondering about Quent and if she'd see him, she gave the thought a swift kick from her mind.

"What are you scowling about?" Lettie asked as she bustled through, heading toward the laundry room with a pile of clothes. She didn't wait for an answer. "Cassie," she said, pausing beside the table, "you are going to have to buy some more jeans. Why, all yours are getting so faded and thin." She shook the pile, indicating the pants on the top. "On second thought, why don't you buy yourself a few skirts or dresses. If I didn't know you better, I'd wonder if you had real legs."

Cassie laughed. "Yes, I can just see me loading feed sacks for the customers in a skirt. And I have dresses, Lettie, just not much occasion other than church for wearing them. It's impractical for me to spend money on clothes I'd hardly wear."

"If you ask me, you could stand a bit more impracticality, girl." Lettie gave her an all-knowing look. "Oh—Jesse said to tell you instead of working at the store this afternoon, he'd catch a ride home and fix that break in the fence you've been hollering about." At Cassie's wide-eyed surprise, Lettie said softly, "He's growing up, Cassie."

Cassie shook her head softly. Yes, Jesse was growing up. A man, nearly. Before too many more years, both Springer and Jesse would have families of their own. The thought left a hollow spot within her heart.

She rose and began clearing the dishes. There was too much to be done for her to be sitting there mooning over life or recalling her stupidity in kissing Quentin Hatfield last night, she thought, shutting the memory behind a door she intended to keep closed.

She was having nothing to do with that type of man. She wouldn't be one of his many women. She thought of the gun at Springer's hip that morning. That was Quent's life, too. She would have nothing to do with it!

She called a repair man for the washer, then just couldn't resist calling Anita at the hospital and hearing every tiny detail about "their" baby.

Cork was waiting in the back of the truck for her. Cassie stopped to pet him, marveling as always at how the hound knew it was a weekday. On six days, Monday through Saturday, Cassie drove in to Doyle City to the feed store. And on five of those six days Cork waited in the back of her pickup truck to go along. He skipped Saturday. And since he'd formed the habit, he'd never made a mistake. It was sort of comforting.

Slipping behind the wheel, Cassie gave a sigh. She might as well be prepared for a lot of talking today. Doyle City was a small town; by now most of its inhabitants had heard about Anita's emergency and would be wanting to hear every minute deal, again and again. She grinned, thinking of Quent repeating the story—he'd be called on to do it until he'd want to hide, she'd bet. Her smile remained as she recalled the foolish look on his face last night when he'd held a brand new life in his hands. Then, unbidden, even unwanted, she again remembered his kiss.

She shook the picture from her mind. She did not intend to keep thinking of Quentin Hatfield. That kiss was a result of the magic still lingering from sharing Q.C.'s birth.

They had been warm and glowing from all that, and it had just sort of caused...well, caused them to kiss, she thought vaguely. That's all it had been.

Chapter Four

It was late Friday afternoon, an hour from closing time at the Marlow Feed and Grain. Muffled noise came from the back where Grover O'dell loaded an order of fertilizer and seed for a customer. Cassie was speaking to Anita on the phone.

"You should have seen him." Anita laughed, speaking of Quent. "He stayed up here a full two hours last night, talking to Perry and holding little Q.C. The baby slept the whole time, but it didn't seem to bother Quent."

Cassie hadn't seen Quent since they'd parted that eventful Sunday night. But she'd heard about him enough from both Springer and Anita, and nearly everyone else she ran into in town.

"Are you really going to stick that child with the name of Q.C.?" she asked, changing the subject.

"Yes—Perry and I think it's cute. And it fits him," Anita said, going on into tales of the baby, what he was doing, which wasn't much, and how much fun he was.

Cassie had found time to see him each day and enjoyed every word of her godchild, as Anita and Perry had decided he would be. Quent would be the godfather, which made Cassie a little nervous. Somehow it implied a close link that she didn't care to have. The fact that she and Quent had been together that night helping Anita had also become a topic of speculation in town, a speculation that Cassie had been quick to squelch.

"We'll be at the party tonight for a little bit," Anita told her finally. "Not too long, 'cause we don't want to keep Q.C. out. Cassie, are you going to have ice cream tonight?"

Cassie laughed. "Are you still craving ice cream?"

"Yes—isn't it awful. And I'm supposed to be on a diet."

"Yes, I'll have ice cream," Cassie promised. "Now, I've got to run. I'll see you later."

Cassie added ice cream to the list of things needed from the grocery store, grabbed her purse and went to the back to find Grover. He was leaning against the open bay door, his arms crossed over his overalls, his red ball cap askew, his eyes closed in his grizzled face and his cheeks puffed with tobacco. Grover O'dell was a nice, gentle man, but definitely one of a kind. Cork, his head pillowed on Grover's foot, perked his ears, as much as Cork ever perked, and that wasn't much.

"Grover," Cassie said softly, fearful of startling him. She chuckled inwardly. Nothing startled Grover. Slowly he opened his eyes. "I'm leaving now. Did Donner pay for the load?"

"Half," Grover said. "Didn't think it polite to say anything."

Cassie sighed, giving a small smile. "Half is fine—no, we don't want to say anything. Donner has enough troubles at the present." Most of it of his own causing, she added to herself.

"So I heard," Grover grunted. "I'll close up. See you tomorree."

Coaxing Cork into standing and following, Cassie headed for her truck. Glancing at her watch, she complained to Springer in her head. He had arranged the party. He had invited half the country. But he couldn't be bothered to help with the arrangements. He'd laughed at her this morning, saying he'd done his part: he'd done the inviting.

Walking down the sidewalk to the bank, Cassie passed the dress shop. Idly she glanced through the window, and a skirt caught her eye. It had earth-tone Indian designs stitched around it. Cassie paused, wondering. Then she shook her head. She was in a rush. Besides, she could just wear her jeans tonight. They would do.

When she came out of the bank, she found herself standing in front of the dress-shop window again. The skirt beckoned, and she went inside.

Holding it against her, Cassie looked in the mirror. The skirt was fine wool flannel, full and long in the style of the moment, and feminine with intricate Indian embroidery.

"That's an original, Cassie. Handmade, one of a kind," Rose Wheeler said, watching.

"It's beautiful," Cassie breathed. Practicality raised its head. "Oh—I don't know. I really need a new pair of jeans." Observing her reflection again, she ran her fingers over the skirt.

Her gaze moved to her face. How long, she wondered, had it been since she'd worn makeup? There was just never any time. Or much reason. And who would notice? Springer? Jesse? The cows?

"I think I'll take it," she told Rose, swinging away from the mirror.

"This belt would set it off." Smiling, Rose laid a belt of thin leather woven through carved silver disks beside the skirt on the counter. "Especially with this sweater."

When Cassie emerged from the shop, she held all three in packages beneath her arms, and she was scolding herself for her impracticality. She could have bought five pairs of sturdy jeans with the money. Cork's droopy eyes seemed to agree as he peered at her through the back window of the truck.

"Mind your own business," Cassie muttered, starting the truck.

* * *

Most of the guests arrived on time and seemed to be enjoying themselves. Cassie was so glad she'd splurged and bought the outfit. She'd brushed her long hair up into a loose coil, for once giving thanks for the curls that femininely framed her face. Jesse had whistled his approval when he saw her. She'd received numerous compliments and several stunned looks. Embarrassment niggled at Cassie—did she usually look so plain and dowdy? Or was she simply extraordinarily pretty tonight?

For about the hundredth time Cassie looked at the clock. The party had been going on for almost two hours—not only without the host, but also without the guest of honor. Springer and Quent had yet to show up. Nor had they called.

I'm not going to worry, Cassie told herself. Those two are together, and whatever mischief they're up to certainly doesn't deserve worry. Yet, the dark image of a gun played upon her thoughts. She continually looked at the darkened windows, but all they showed her was her own reflection.

Moving through the softly lit living room, she picked up empty glasses and spoke to the guests. The large room was relatively quiet. A low fire burned in the fireplace. People sat in groups, talking. Bill Thayer and Owen Payne played checkers.

In the hallway it was noisier, and the music was louder because Jesse had moved the speakers into the dining room. At the present a slow pop-country tune played. Several couples danced on the hardwood floor of the dimly lit hallway and into the dining room. Cassie noticed Jesse and Linda Jones among them, holding each other close. A single hair between them would be squished, she thought. She very briefly considered breaking them apart, but her common sense prevailed against humiliating her brother that way. Linda was a nice girl—not the girl who wrote that outlandish note—and the two were among a group of people. Not much more than a bit of hugging could go on. Still, she vowed to keep an eye on Jesse. He was a Marlow, after all, and considerably resourceful.

The dining room table had been moved up against the wall and laden with sandwiches, nuts, sweets and potato chips. Two wide coolers on legs provided soft drinks and beer, and two coffee makers steamed away.

The kitchen was bright and considerably noisier, rowdy with the talk and laughter of men. A poker game was in progress at the table, and two young men were arm wrestling at the corner of the counter. Cassie made her way to the freezer for ice. Someone called for her to join the poker game, but she declined. "Don't want to take all your money," she teased. Several voices challenged her, but she just shook her head, her eyes straying to the window.

Where were they? Surely they would come any minute.

As if in answer to her plea, a truck's headlights appeared down the road, then another right behind the first. From the living room someone called, "They're here!"

Cassie stood beneath the side porch light and watched both men get out from their trucks. Springer let out a loud "whooee!" and smiled widely. Several men from the house went to meet them, and a lot of congenial backslapping went on.

Cassie quivered inside. Thank God they were all right. Her gaze moved from Springer to Quent and lingered. He was smiling that slow smile. His shoulders were wide beneath a tan western-cut sport coat, and his shirt was open at the neck. Denim jeans stretched tightly over his slim hips.

Then Springer was walking toward her, and snatches of comments came to her. Springer had been in some sort of fracas. She saw he had a nasty scratch across his jaw, and his uniform bore traces of mud. Her stomach knotted, and her breath caught. He could have been hurt.

He was smiling broadly. People surrounded him and Quent, men mostly, all talking. Cassie stood aside as they headed for the kitchen.

"Sorry I'm late, Sis," Springer tossed to her on his way into the house. "Had a bit of trouble." His eyes twinkled as they asked for forgiveness. Cassie cast him a quick smile before the demands of others bore him into the kitchen. "Man, I need a beer," she heard him say, and then the voices blended together. She caught sight of Quent's pale hat above the heads in the light as he streamed along with the others into the house.

She was left alone on the long side porch. Turning slowly, she went to the very end and leaned against the post, crossing her arms against the chill and gazing out at the darkening meadow.

Springer had been in a fight, hadn't been killed but he could have been. And Quent was in on it. His duty didn't even start officially until Monday, but he couldn't stay out of it. Two hard-handed heroes returning majestically from the wars.

Cassie looked forlornly down at her new skirt. It wasn't good, she thought. She was thinking far too much of Quent. She cared far too much what he thought of her. No, it wasn't good. She was so mixed up, she didn't even know what her true feelings were.

Laughter sounded from the house. He was in there now, no doubt surrounded by friends—women. He hadn't even looked her way.

What had she been expecting from tonight, anyway? A little fun, she guessed. For some strange reason she felt rather like she'd been expecting a rich, creamy chocolate shake but had sipped the straw and found vanilla.

The screen door behind her creaked as someone came out. She heard the scrape of a boot on the wood flooring but didn't turn around. It was probably someone leaving, or just out for air. Maybe they'd go away.

"Seems as if I remember a little girl that used to love orange soda. Does this pretty lady?"

Hearing the timbre of Quent's voice, Cassie whirled to see him standing under the yellow porch light. He was hatless, and the light played upon his golden-brown hair, loose strands of which fell across his forehead.

The easy smile beneath his mustache slipped, and his eyes narrowed as his gaze moved from her face slowly downward, then quickly back up. Giving a crooked smile, he walked lazily toward her. Her heart fluttered, and she felt foolishly pleased, for she saw appreciation written on his face. He thought her pretty—the one man whom she'd hoped would. And, enjoying the moment, she ignored the warning sounding within her heart.

Quent had caught a glimpse of Cassie through the kitchen window. He'd been looking all over the kitchen for her, pressed among the crowd of men and women offering their greetings. He was nearest to the refrigerator when someone called to him for a beer. While getting the beer, he'd spied the bottles of soft drinks, remembering how Cassie had loved orange soda as a child. Pulling out the soft drinks, he'd gradually inched his way to the kitchen door and somehow, miraculously, had managed to slip out the door unobserved.

He hadn't expected Cassie to look like this, not this feminine, this beautiful, this sexy. Her sweater was loose, large, the kind women have been favoring, the material falling soft and low over her full breasts. Cassie-fashion, her hands were dipped casually into the pockets of the skirt that flowed nicely over her hips and well past her knees. There was a sensuous aura about her, yet he could tell she had no idea of it, which made her all the more enticing for a man.

His eyes were again drawn to her lips as he walked toward her. Carrying two soft drink bottles, he held one toward her. She smiled, her eyes warm.

"Thanks," she said softly. "You remembered." There was surprise in her voice.

Quent looked down into her wide eyes. "I remember a lot." He waited for her reaction. She just kept looking at him, and he wondered if she remembered that day. He couldn't tell anything by her expression. "It's crowded in there," he said, indicating the kitchen. She nodded in answer, and he saw her shiver slightly. "And cold out here," he added. "Here, use my coat."

"No—then you'll be cold," she protested as he handed her his bottle so he could slip from his coat. "We'll just go in."

"Hell, no," he grumbled. "I need some room to breathe. There." He settled his coat over her shoulders, allowing his hands to brush the bare skin above her sweater. It was warm.

Turning away from him, she sipped her soft drink. She didn't say anything. Quent watched her, wanting to talk to her.

"I'm sorry we were late," he said.

She shrugged. "It couldn't be helped. Everyone seemed to be having a good time, even without you two."

Quent chuckled with her, then took a swallow from his bottle. "You weren't worried, I hope."

A shadow flickered across her features. She had been worried, he saw with a twinge of surprise. He thought fleetingly of her father.

"Not much," she denied. "Springer's always late. If I remember correctly, he was born two weeks late, and has been running behind time ever since." Her laugh had a deep tone in it for a woman, and Quent liked it. "I thought you weren't supposed to start duty until Monday," she said.

"I was the one handy—and don't let that scratch on Springer's jaw bother you. We happened, totally by accident, to come upon two guys butchering a deer they'd just shot. They ran, and Springer took off after them, falling over a log in the process. But they ended up coming along peacefully."

Cassie laughed. "Springer won't appreciate you letting the cat out of the bag. Bet he's in there now telling a bit of a different tale." Her face was soft in the dim light, her skin like cream.

Something fell against his foot. Looking down, Quent saw a hound dog flopped onto his boots. "What's this?" He looked at Cassie. He hadn't heard the dog come up.

She was laughing. "That's Cork. Apparently, he likes you. He does that to everyone he likes."

"Is that so?" Quent moved his feet, and the dog gave him a reproachful look.

"That, and you have root beer. Cork loves root beer."

"Oh." Quent bent to stroke the dog and poured a puddle of root beer near the dog's mouth. Without rising from his prone position, the hound began to lap up the sweet liquid.

Cassie bent down beside him. "See?" she said. "But he doesn't like orange soda." She poured a bit to prove her point, and the dog sniffed but ignored it.

Her head was close; Quent caught the scent of her, fresh, like roses with the morning dew upon them. With gentle strokes, she ran her hand along the dog's fur. She looked up into Quent's eyes, and attraction sparked between them, so strong that Quent felt he could touch it. Her eyes were dark in the dim light, and grew large. He was going to kiss her and knew that she knew it, but he hesitated for fear she'd pull away as she had last time.

The kitchen door opened, and laughter poured from the house. Quent didn't know if it was that, or if Cassie didn't want the kiss. But suddenly she moved back and stood up. Quent rose beside her just as Anita stepped out the door. *Damn*, he thought. *So damn many people everywhere!*

"I've been looking...for you two." Anita's words slowed as her gaze moved curiously from Cassie to Quent. "Perry and I are going to leave in a few minutes. But we couldn't go without having little Q.C. tell his godparents goodbye."

Leaving Cork on the porch after Quent had poured a fresh puddle of root beer for the hound, they joined the merrymaking going on inside the house. On his way to see the baby, Quent was waylaid by April Sewell and another young woman whom he wasn't sure he knew. She acted as though she knew him, though, so Quent was polite. They were pretty women, definitely flirting with him with wide eyes, deliberately brushing against him, asking about his helicopter and if he would take them up sometime.

Quent smiled, trying without being rude, to extricate himself and join Cassie. Glancing around, he found her. She stood holding little Q.C. close, rubbing her cheek against his head. The picture she made pleased him.

Quent came up behind her. Cassie's senses pricked at his nearness. Why in the world was he standing so close? His coat brushed against her back. Smiling, she bid Anita and Perry and the baby a polite goodbye. Quent's mellow tones echoed behind her.

Purposely keeping her eyes and thoughts from Quent, she stepped toward the living room, intent on seeing to the guests. Let Quent return to the ladies who had so held his rapt attention, she thought primly.

When his strong hand closed around her wrist, she looked up in surprise.

"Come dance with me," he said quietly, his smile cajoling.

"But I need to—"

He cut her off. "You don't need to do anything. These people are old enough to take care of themselves. And it is Springer's party." He laughed, pulling her into the hall, his arms closing loosely around her as he led her two-stepping to the lively music.

"It's yours, too," Cassie said, raising her voice above the music.

"Ah, but I'm the guest of honor. I can do anything I want."

His eyes twinkled down at her. He moved with a fluid rhythm, whisking her smoothly around the hall, expertly dodging the other few couples. Cassie's heart picked up speed. She enjoyed the free-flowing motion. Quent's brown eyes twinkled down at her, enticing her, daring her to have fun. One of his hands was firm and hot upon her waist, the other rough and strong around her hand. She caught the inviting scent of his cologne.

He's an old friend being kind, she told herself. That's all.

The music ended, and Cassie broke away, but Quent kept a firm hold on her hand. She didn't have time to wonder at the actions as the strains of a slow song began, and he pulled her to him. Cassie found her chin near his shoulder, her hand beneath his jacket at his waist. His muscles were firm beneath his shirt, and his body was warm.

She was amazed to find herself in this position. What was Quent thinking? What in the world was she thinking? Nervously she pushed herself away from him to put some distance between them, to dance a friendly dance with an old and dear friend.

But Quent held her tightly. He brushed his thighs against hers and rubbed his chin softly against her hair. It felt so good. Just for now, Cassie thought, involuntarily relaxing against him as she gave in to the delicious yearnings of her body. Instantly Quent's arms tightened around her. She felt his belt buckle pressing into her as he moved seductively against her.

Heat raced through her veins. *Just for now.* The thought was hazy in her mind. Her breath came fast. Her attention focused on the warmth emanating from the strong male body moving rhythmically against her. Her body and mind slipped into a glowing world of pleasing sensations, and she savored them.

Then gradually Cassie became fully aware of where she was—and that the music had stopped. Voices murmured around her. And Quent still held her close, with his body hot against hers!

She pushed herself back and jerked her hand from his waist. "I..." She looked at him, searching his eyes. They were dark with heat, Cassie saw in wonder. And he plainly wasn't looking at her in a friendly fashion. He continued to look at her, leaving no doubt as to his thoughts.

It was the same way he'd looked at her that day so long ago. The time when he'd kissed her. And Cassie found her gaze moving to his lips, which were half hidden beneath a thick gold-tinged mustache, and wondering what their kiss would be like now.

"Quent!"

The call startled them both. Turning quickly, Cassie saw April Sewell approaching. With a smile that was all for Quent, April dismissed Cassie with barely a glance.

"Quent," April purred. "Y'all come in the kitchen. Springer's got a hot poker game going. He wants you to join in. And I'm good luck." Putting a proprietary hand at Quent's elbow, she gave Cassie a pointed look. "You don't mind, now do you, Cassie?"

You had to hand it to April, Cassie thought. Nothing daunted the woman's audacity. It struck Cassie then that she was being put into a position of vying for a man—for Quent. And she didn't like the idea at all! She was not, by any stretch of the imagination, a romantic interest for Quent. She had more common sense.

Quent gave April his lazy smile. "That sounds interesting," he said, his gaze traveling thoughtfully to Cassie.

"Don't lose your shirt," Cassie teased lightly, stepping away.

But Quent clamped his hand on her wrist, and he pulled her back. His eyes twinkling, he tucked her very close into the crook of his arm.

"Does Cassie still play poker?" He raised a questioning eyebrow. "As I remember, she could play very well—and I helped teach her."

"As I remember," Cassie said, "I used to beat you and Mike often."

His gaze challenged her. "Think you could still do it?"

She looked at him. The teasing light was in his eyes again, the mood like it'd been when they were kids, easy, familiar, daring—no longer threatening. And his grin enticed her to grin back.

"I've no doubt I could," she answered smugly. Just like when they were children—she couldn't refuse a dare.

"Then I guess you'll have to prove it," he said smoothly, escorting both Cassie and April before him. April pouted, but Cassie hid a smile. She was going to beat the socks off him.

Room was made for them at the table. Hiding her nervousness, Cassie sat down quietly, trying not to call attention to herself. She wasn't used to playing with people other than her brothers and a few of their close friends. And then she didn't play often. She used to, though, years ago with Mike and Quent.

Hadley Smith, who had played several times with her, turned in his cards, grumbling, "I'm getting out. I've lost enough already without playing against Cassie. Damn angel sits on her shoulder." Springer laughed, and the others cast her covert curious glances.

She sat demurely, picking up the cards dealt her, one by one. An angel sitting on her shoulder couldn't have looked more innocent, she decided. And she wasn't all that threatening. It was Mike and Springer who'd started the rumor several years ago about her playing ability. Yes, she could play well, but she was no card shark. She allowed a small inward sigh. Though it did seem as if an angel watched over her because she always got dealt wonderfully good hands. No, it wasn't ability—it was luck, plain and simple. And when you had it, you had it, though she tried not to get carried away with pride.

"Two, please," she said, trading in two cards to Springer, who'd dealt. She smiled sweetly at Quent, and he smiled back. Leaning on his shoulder, April cast a fleeting triumphant glance at Cassie. Then bending close, she whispered into Quent's ear and smiled seductively. When Quent smiled back, Cassie averted her gaze. Men, she thought irritably. Any fool could see that April was deliberately pressing her hip against Quent's shoulder, though she kept her expression perfectly innocent. There was nothing, Cassie thought emphatically, innocent about April Sewell.

The room seemed to have become quieter, and Cassie self-consciously felt that people were watching her.

Springer won the first hand. Smiling expansively, he raked the coins toward him. They played with real money, but used only nickels, dimes and quarters.

Cassie won the next two hands. As she raked in the small pile of coins the second time, Quent smiled at her. Suddenly suspicious, Cassie wondered if he'd allowed her to win. Mentally she went back over the hands. No, she decided positively, she'd simply been lucky again.

Quent rose and left his chair. A moment later Cassie looked up to see him placing an orange soda in front of her. His eyes were warm upon her. She just looked at him and blinked, unable to understand the impressions she was receiving. April remained at his shoulder, yet he hadn't brought her back anything to drink. And at the moment April was staring hotly at Cassie. Cassie looked down at her cards.

This particular evening her luck held true to form. Cassie won often, about half the time. Quent was the other heavy winner. But then, he'd been the one to teach her the game in the first place; their playing habits were evenly matched.

Then it was as if the angel on her shoulder got tired of fooling around and decided to get serious, for Cassie began winning—and winning.

She tried to keep the smile from her lips but couldn't. There was just something about betting—even pennies—and winning. Something that charged the human spirit. She was having such fun! Adrenaline pumped through her as she decided which cards to play, waited anxiously, then found in that wonderful moment of truth that she'd won. There was something stupendous about doing it again and again.

And, Cassie admitted, the edge that made it so special was playing against Quent—and winning against him.

It was dangerous, the feelings she was having for Quent. Every time he looked at her, she felt a throb begin deep in the recesses of her body and flow through her limbs. Again and again her gaze was drawn to his. She studied him, and wondered.

Finally only Quent and Cassie played. It had grown quite late, and except for those few in the kitchen, the guests had left, April Sewell among them, to Cassie's smothered delight. Jesse, his eyes growing droopy, sat on a stool near the counter, eating a sandwich. Springer and a few of his close friends were standing around the table, talking, idly watching the game, wondering if Quent's luck would change, or if he'd simply give in.

Cassie wondered, too.

"I think I must call it quits," she said, hiding the reluctance she felt under a casual smile. She really didn't want to leave. She wanted to stay where Quent was, but that was stupid, she told herself. Of course she wanted to leave. She was tired. "You all can stay up all night, but I have to work tomorrow."

There were a few groans, a few agreements.

"One more hand, Cass," Quent said in his mellow tone. "I want one more chance." His eyes twinkled mischievously. "I'll bet all my change... plus a kiss against your entire pot there."

Cassie looked at him and blinked. Her gaze moved to his lips, then back to his eyes. They were daring her. Her pulse sounded loudly within her ears, and she was conscious that it had grown very quiet in the room. Glancing at Springer, she saw him watching her closely.

How silly, she thought. Nothing to make a big deal about. And she certainly wasn't going to have anyone thinking it was a big deal. Yet she'd grown very warm. Quent's tone made one simple little kiss, one simple little bet, sound like so much more.

Chapter Five

Okay,'' Cassie said, giving a casual shrug, looking at no one in particular.

It was just a simple little bet, and she was bound to win; she'd won the last three hands in a row. Besides, if she lost, she'd only be losing a total of maybe eight dollars and a little kiss. It was the challenge Quent was after—that natural challenge that drew anyone to betting. How foolish of us humans, she thought with a wry inward grin, knowing she was touched by the same strange affliction.

She was beginning to understand how Mike, Springer, and their friends could stay up until the early hours of the morning playing as they did. It wasn't for money; the most anyone won was eight to ten dollars. It was the thrill they experienced, she knew, from what they considered a skill, and what Cassie always thought of as luck.

A little kiss. That was all. Pictures and sensations from long ago flashed through her memory, intertwined with new imaginings . . . should she lose.

Her gaze was drawn to Quent's. His eyes twinkled as if he knew something she didn't.

A kiss, she thought wryly. It was just the sort of bet Quentin or one of her brothers would make. And somehow he managed to make it seem substantial, the one bet of a lifetime. It was his way, as was her brothers', to live every moment to the hilt, as though it would be their last. The air fairly crackled; everyone's attention drawn to the table, anxious to see if Cassie would beat Quent. If her incredible luck would hold.

She lifted the cards Springer dealt her one by one—queen of clubs, jack of clubs, ten of hearts, king of clubs. Her heart picked up speed. Six of diamonds. Her gaze went over the cards. King, queen, jack, all of clubs. She wanted to smile. The angel still sat on her shoulder.

Quent looked at her, and she looked back. They each managed to keep perfectly blank poker faces.

She returned the ten and six to Springer, receiving two cards in return. She touched them, not looking at them as Quent turned in one card.

Cassie picked up the two cards. Looking at them, she felt the blood leave her face and an icy chill run down her spine. The next instant it was all she could do to keep from jumping and yelling. How could her luck run so well? It was nearly a once-in-a-lifetime hand—well, maybe twice-in-cha-lifetime, if one played a lot of poker.

She had drawn a royal flush. Ace, king, queen, jack, ten, all of clubs.

What, she wondered, were the chances of drawing such a hand? They had to be outrageous. It wasn't as though she'd done a thing; she'd simply picked up the cards Springer dealt her—she'd simply picked up a royal flush.

And by doing so, she'd beat Quent.

Careful to keep her "poker face," she looked at him. She'd beat him, could savor it even before he knew. His eyes glittered, but his face remained impassive.

He thinks he's won, Cassie realized. *He must hold an awfully good hand.*

But she had better.

"Call," Quent said, a triumphant smile breaking over his face as he spread his cards on the table.

Good grief, Cassie thought, he did have a good hand. Four of a kind, king's high. He waited, watching her.

Looking into his eyes, she gave a deliberately quiet smile and very slowly spread her cards. The grin slipped from Quent's face to be replaced by a look of incredulity.

"Hot damn!" Hadley Smith let out. "I told you an angel sat on her shoulder."

Jesse peered over her shoulder. Springer shook his head, grinning. "And some people think I exaggerate about Cassie's poker."

Cassie heard them, but her gaze was on Quent, and suddenly she felt her balloon of triumph sinking.

Giving his mellow smile, he inclined his head. "Congratulations, Cass. I guess Mike and I taught you well." However, disappointment showed in his eyes and stabbed Cassie's heart.

Suddenly she didn't feel she'd really won. Suddenly she longed to feel Quent's kiss upon her lips, if only because of a bet.

There came the scraping of chairs as the men rose. "Thanks, Cassie." "Good hand, Cassie." "Thanks, Springer." "Good night."

Cassie nodded, smiling automatically. Averting her gaze, she began clearing the table as the men trooped outside. Jesse bid good-night.

Finding an empty coffee can, Cassie raked her winnings into it. Springer would likely need the change next time he played. She replaced the cards into their box, then threw them back on the table as if they were at fault for her feelings of frustration.

Pulling a tray from the cabinet, she strode purposefully into the living room. The fire in the fireplace had burned out, and the room was cool. She shut the glass doors of the fireplace, then began cleaning up the party leavings.

What in the world, she fumed, was the matter with her? She'd won, hadn't she? And with the best hand in the world. A poker hand people dream about.

But she was angry. What a stupid bet for Quent to make!

And she wished he'd won. He'd been so disappointed to lose the final hand, and she wished she'd had a chance, just this once, to feel his lips on hers. To find out what it would be like to really kiss him again.

No, she didn't! she told herself emphatically. It had been a silly little bet, and she'd won. She was tired; that was all. The anger slipped away, replaced by fatigue. Yes, she was tired . . . that was all.

"I wanted to thank you for the party, Cass." Hearing Quent's voice, she jumped, then turned to see him standing just inside the room. "I'm sorry." He gave a small grin. "I didn't mean to startle you."

"That's okay," she tossed at him, unable to look into his face. "And we enjoyed the party, too."

Out of the corner of her eye she saw him sweep several soft drink bottles from an end table. He brought them toward her, saying, "You should have Springer do this. As I understand it, the party was his idea."

Cassie bent to gather empty glasses. "Yes, but he has yet to clean up after anything in this house."

Quent stood very close. "Maybe it's time you let him do more. If you don't do it, maybe he will." There was gentle criticism in his tone. "Don't you think it's time you quit picking up after him, Cass?"

Cassie looked at him sharply, but her retort was cut off when he pressed his lips to hers. At the same time his arms clamped hard around her.

Amazed, Cassie stopped breathing, and her mind whirled. Then she pushed furiously against his hard chest, outraged at his audacity. Immediately Quent lifted his head. He loosened his hold, but his arms remained around her.

Looking up at him, Cassie stilled. The planes of his face were taut, expressionless. But not his eyes. They glowed with heat, and his gaze seemed to caress her face, speaking plainly of his desire, his questioning. She was drawn by those eyes, as a cat to a warm spot in the sun. Longing flickered deep within her, growing to a strong pulsing. Involuntarily her gaze moved to his lips. Her hand twitched to touch his mustache and see if it was as soft as it looked. Would his lips be firm upon hers?

Then very slowly his lips moved toward her. Watching, Cassie saw them part. She drew in a sharp breath as by instinct her own lips opened, waiting, anticipating. He smelled of manly cologne and night dew. She caught the faint taste of root beer as his tongue flicked into her mouth, and he drew upon her tongue.

Cassie lost herself in the sweetness of his kiss, wanting desperately to savor all she could of the sensations flowing in waves throughout her body. And to savor all she could of the man responsible for the wonder. She strained to pull him even closer. He was hard against her, so hard, so firm. Yet the strong cords of his neck trembled tenderly beneath her fingertips as she stroked his smooth skin, her fingers moving into the thick, silky pelt of his hair.

Cassie trembled beneath his touch as Quent rubbed his hands slowly down her back, pressing her hard against him. Her waist felt so small. He lightened his touch, afraid of hurting her smaller frame. She moved against him. And still he kissed her, drugged by her sensuous response, a response that sent the heat flaming within him.

She smelled of warm summer nights and felt soft and pliable. The girl he'd remembered had turned into a full-fledged woman. Now her breasts pressed against his chest, and he felt her rubbing them slightly against him.

Need, desire, heat, burst over him like an exploding star. Dragging his lips from hers, Quent fought for air. He held her to him, savoring the feel of her silky hair and her feminine form. He moved to bend his legs, an inner instinct compelling him downward, and he thought only of lying beside her, only of touching her. Within his mind he imagined her skin creamy white and soft beneath his touch; he had no thought of time or where they were.

Gradually it came to him that she was pushing him away, that she was softly struggling. He let her go and looked down to see anguish written across her face. Her eyes were wide in horror.

"Cassie..." Quent reached to draw her near again, wanting to ease the pain he saw on her face, to understand it.

She stepped back. Her lips moved, but no words came out. Then she turned, hurried away from him and out of the room. Her steps sounded light and rapid upon the carpeted stairs.

Stunned, Quent stared at the empty archway. His heart pounded, his body struggling to attain some sense of norm, yet aching with desire.

What had he done? he wondered in frustration. She'd liked it; he knew she had. *Then why had she run away?*

Well, he'd find out, Quent thought hotly, taking two strides across the room, then stopping. He raked a hand through his hair, considering uncertainly. No one ever got anywhere by being demanding with Cassie. And she'd been scared, hurt, or something.

It had been a big surprise to him, too, he considered. Just like that time nine years ago. Now, just as then, it had been like two fiery suns colliding. The reaction between them was so powerful that Quent wasn't sure he could comprehend it even now. It was something he'd never experienced—except with Cassie. And this time he wasn't doubting it. He knew it was real. And yet it was frightening in its intensity.

But, damn it! They weren't the children they'd been then!

Again he considered going to her. He'd have to pound on her door, no doubt. But what if that just drove her farther from him?

And what if she didn't feel the same way he did? The thought cut him raggedly. He dismissed it, but it returned. Just because he felt this way, was no reason she should. Maybe she had that kind of passionate reaction to any man who kissed her. Thinking of another man kissing her angered him.

"Hey, Quent, you still here?" Springer said from the doorway. "Where's Cass?"

Quent looked up, blinking, bringing his mind back to the present. "Darned if I know," he ground out angrily. "Good night." Striding around Springer, he fairly stomped from the house.

Cassie sat at the open window of her darkened bedroom, the fresh fall air cool against her burning cheeks. A half moon darkly lit the cedar trees in the meadow beyond their yard. Faintly, from the drive on the other side of the house, she heard an engine start. The sound roared unnecessarily hard, and she imagined Quent's truck going down the drive. Gradually the sound faded into the night.

A few moments later Springer's tread sounded up the stairs and paused at her door. There came a light tap. "Cassie?"

She stilled, deciding not to answer, feeling a twinge of guilt in making the decision, but she was unable to face him at the moment.

"Cassie?" Springer said again. Several seconds later his footsteps retreated in the direction of his room.

She wondered if Quent had said anything to him, wondered if he worried about her.

When something light and cool touched her hand, Cassie realized she was crying. Her tears came in earnest then. Quickly she pulled at the quilt around her and buried her face into its folds to muffle her sobs. Thankfully, her brothers' rooms were on the opposite side of the hall.

After several minutes she managed to stop the sobs. She'd never been a woman to cry much. It did little but stuff up her nose and make her feel worse. And now she felt no release in the action; her body still throbbed, crying out for Quent's touch.

She didn't want this, she thought, pounding her clenched fist into the blanket. She didn't want to feel this way about Quentin Hatfield. She didn't think she wanted to feel this way about anyone. Even thinking of it now fairly took her breath away.

When he touched her, she forgot who she was. She forgot everything. She lost herself. It was frightening, much too powerful. Never had she felt such…such passion. Her face burned as she thought of the word. And her mind whispered, yes, yes, she had. Nine years ago, that hot summer day at the river, in Quent's arms.

Her mind wandered and slipped into remembering that time and the moments before in the living room. It was wonderful, she thought softly, reluctantly, curiously. Did everyone in the world feel this way at some time in life? Oh, how dreadful if not! It was wonderful, she decided.

Did Quent feel the same? Did he feel as though he'd lost control and was vulnerable in those moments? Surely he didn't; he was strong and sure of himself. He was also familiar with women. No doubt he knew exactly what he was doing when he made love to a woman.

No, Cassie thought, I do not intend to get involved with Quentin Hatfield. It would be far too dangerous.

It occurred to her that the danger was probably what added to the excitement of it all. Since the beginning of time, women have been attracted to the daring, dashing, adventurous type of man. Look at the women who flocked around her brothers. Heaven knew why. It didn't make a bit of sense. All those women who were attracted by such men also wanted them to settle down and behave once they captured them.

Well, it just didn't work. Cassie knew that firsthand. The intelligent thing to do was to start with a settled, commonsense sort of man in the first place. One who would be home in bed beside her every night of their married life. And if he did have to be away, it would be for some nice, safe business trip—not on a stake out for criminals or pulling people from flood waters or some wild adventure he'd thought up.

But would she feel the same wonderful abandoned passion with such a man? Could she, her mind whispered, ever feel it with anyone other than Quent?

Of course she could. She never had, but surely, somewhere out there was the right man for her. Passion faded. Good secure love didn't. And that was what she wanted.

Besides, she thought, moving to turn on the bedside lamp and get undressed, her life was very full. Yes, full of men. Springer and Jesse, even Mike when he'd come home to visit. She listened to their problems and applauded their escapades. Her life was full of those three. Why would she need Quent?

The answer came as she looked at the wide expanse of the double bed. Who took care of her when she needed it? Who listened to her problems and shared her joys?

Pushing those thoughts from her mind, she jerked a nightgown over her head. Her life was perfectly fine. She didn't need any man such as Quentin Hatfield.

She admitted that it may not be easy to drive him from her mind. But she could do it. She was of strong character with a hearty self-discipline. She had no intention of becoming even in the least involved with Quentin Hatfield. She would not spend her life as her mother had, dying a little more each day as she wondered if her man would come home. It was enough with her brothers.

It was one of those clear mid-November days peculiar to Oklahoma, where the sky was crystal blue, seemed close enough to touch, and a near-warm breeze blew. Cassie even had a window open in the kitchen. She hummed as she mixed cookie batter. Jesse was at a friend's house, riding his three-wheeler, and Springer was on duty somewhere; nevertheless, a male had her attention—little Q.C. He slept in a small portable crib set atop the table.

After sliding a pan of cookies into the oven, she peered at him, adjusting his blanket across a bare toe. It was hard to believe he was two weeks old today. Wasn't it just yesterday Quent had held him before her?

Tires crunched upon the drive, and Cassie moved to the door to see who it was. She didn't expect Jesse, and who knew when Springer would show up. Recognizing the beige pickup and the tall frame that slipped from the cab, Cassie's heart raced. It was Quent.

She hadn't seen him all week and was pleased that she'd kept him from her thoughts. But here he was now, and all she could think of was the last time she'd seen him—the abandoned way she'd kissed him, the humiliating way she'd fled. What must he think?

Whirling from the window, for an insane instant she considered not answering the door and hiding. But of course that was impossible; Quent could see plainly through the window in the kitchen door, and there was Q.C.

And what in the world was she thinking? She couldn't hide from him forever. She'd have to face him sometime. It might as well be here and now, without a lot of observers. Yes, they were alone. Oh, she wailed inwardly, maybe she'd rather have a lot of observers.

Composing her face, she went to the door and opened it.

"Hello, Quent." She gave a friendly smile. "I'm sorry, Springer's out on duty." Of course he'd know that. It was a stupid thing to say. But then why was he here? The puzzling thought came suddenly.

It was unnerving, the way he stood quite still, looking at her for a long second before saying anything. And to add to it, Cassie felt a tingling awareness of his closeness sweep across her body.

"I didn't come to see Springer," he said, giving a slow smile. "Or Jesse." His gaze told her pointedly he'd come to see her.

Why, Cassie wondered, was he doing this? Did he want to tease her? Could he actually be interested in her? Surely not....

"Do I smell cookies?" he asked.

"Oh!" Whirling from the door, Cassie ran to the oven. The cookies weren't burned, thankfully. Using a hot pad, she carried the pan to the counter.

"What's this?" Quent looked down into the portable crib.

"Perry took Anita into Chickasha shopping for clothes," Cassie said over her shoulder. "Just for a few hours' break. She can't leave him long since she's nursing."

"And she doesn't want to," Quent added.

"No, she doesn't," Cassie agreed. The heavenly aroma of fresh-baked chocolate chip cookies filled the room. She turned to see Quent fiddling with Q.C.'s cover. "Would you like some cookies?" she asked. She shouldn't have, she thought immediately, but it just came out naturally.

"Especially with a cup of coffee," he said. "I'll make it. Let's see…" He reached easily into a cabinet. "Ah, you still keep the coffee in the same place."

His grin was friendly, the one Cassie remembered from his youth. She relaxed, though quickly averted her eyes as the memory of his kiss lingered. She dropped cookie batter upon the pan with great concentration. She'd been making too much out of his coming out to see her, she thought then. It was only natural for him to come out to their home; he'd done so since he'd been a small boy. Marjean was no doubt getting to him. He was simply doing as he'd done years ago, coming out to relax and enjoy sitting in a chair without plastic on it.

And as for the kiss, well, Quent kissed a lot of women. It was as natural to him as breathing.

"Ah, Cass," Quent said, munching on a warm cookie, "I've never tasted better."

"Thanks. These are still the only thing I can really cook." She sipped from her cup.

Q.C. stirred. Immediately Cassie and Quent looked into the crib. Q.C.'s eyes were open, and his mouth a wide O. He whimpered. Lifting him, Cassie cuddled him to her. "Time for a change," she said.

"Don't look at me," Quent said with a smile, but he was perfectly eager to take Q.C. from her once he'd been changed. "Let's take him out and show him the real world," Quent said. "Trucks, horses, and prairie grass."

"Oh, I don't know, Quent . . ." Cassie hesitated. Somehow it seemed dangerous, taking a small baby outside.

"Come on, Cass. The boy was born in a chopper. He isn't going to die from fresh air. Hand me that blanket."

She helped Quent wrap Q.C. They both laughed at their efforts, finding two pairs of hands clumsier than one. Cassie marveled at the relaxed and perfectly expert way Quent handled the baby.

"You seem right at home with him," she said, unable to keep the surprise from her voice.

"Buddy of mine in Oregon was a single father of three. I used to help him out some," Quent explained. "All small, the youngest six months. His wife died," he said, at Cassie's look. "Here we go, Q.C.; let's acquaint you with the important things in life. Women you already know."

Cassie laughed, her gaze meeting Quent's. Immediately she turned away. The look he'd given her had been purely sensual. Holding the door for Quent, she followed him outside.

She was thoroughly confused, her inner spirit at war. She was attracted to him—*but damn it! She didn't want to be.* She refused to be! *Was he*, she wondered, *actually attracted to her?*

Quent pointed out the two horses in the pasture to Q.C. One became curious and approached them to stick his head over the fence for Cassie to pet. The sun was warm upon her back and shiny upon Quent's golden-brown hair. Q.C. looked content within the crook of his arm.

"Don't you think he's a little young," Cassie said lightly.

"Never too young to be talked to. Look, I'm sure he's interested."

She cast him a skeptical glance, and he laughed his mellow laugh. Cassie found her heart tripped under her ribs at the sound.

"And this is a pickup truck," Quent told Q.C. "You'll have one someday."

Q.C. blinked, squinting in the bright sun. He whimpered and flung out an arm.

"Bring him back in," Cassie told Quent. "I think he's tired of lessons, and he may be hungry. Anita left a bottle."

Quent complied, bringing Q.C. back indoors, and then he insisted on feeding him. Q.C. didn't take to the bottle at first. "He's not used to it," Quent said, gently encouraging the baby. After a few tries Q.C. managed to get the hang of it and sucked eagerly.

Cassie watched Quent holding the tiny child, and her heart warmed. She was surprised, and yet not so. It all fit with the Quent she knew. Then she scolded herself. She certainly didn't need to be having tender thoughts of Quentin Hatfield. She was too confused, too vulnerable. She didn't need to add to it.

Deliberately she turned to cleaning up her baking dishes. Several times she thought she felt Quent's gaze upon her, but she didn't look around to find out.

Q.C. drank about half the bottle, then began crying fretfully. Quent placed him to his shoulder and patted and rocked. When that didn't work, he tried other positions.

"Here, let me," Cassie said, reaching for Q.C. She sat in the rocker, held Q.C. pressed to her breasts as she'd seen Anita do, and rocked. The baby quieted, his eyes closing. In minutes he breathed peacefully in sleep.

When Cassie looked up, she found Quent's thoughtful gaze upon her.

"It's the breasts," he said.

Cassie blinked, stunned and embarrassed. A grin slipped across Quent's face, and she realized he'd seen the discomfiture in her expression.

"Well, it's true, Cass," he said knowingly. "A baby loves a woman's breasts, and yours are—let's just say, more than adequate."

"Thank you, Quentin Hatfield, for your expertise," Cassie said sarcastically. Rising, she turned away from his gaze and gently placed Q.C. back into the small crib.

"Don't tell me, Cass, that with a shape like yours you haven't been complimented by men before," Quent's mellow voice teased.

Cassie refused to answer, mortified that her nipples had hardened. It was his tone, the way he looked at her. She was angry at him and at herself, for heaven help her, she felt pleasure at his roundabout compliment. Reminding herself of Quent's roguish charm, she cooled down.

"Cass," Quent said quietly, "would you like to go to dinner tonight?"

Cassie whirled to face him, unable to hide her surprise. He looked at her, his face a careful mask. He was serious, she saw. The question seemed to hang in the air as her heartbeat pounded in her ears.

Chapter Six

Quent waited for her answer, feeling uncertain, self-conscious, like a teenager asking out the school's head cheerleader. Carefully he made his face a mask, unwilling to let Cassie see.

He'd come out to the Marlow home two times in the past week for the purpose of asking Cassie for a date. Both times, to his extreme irritation, she'd been out, once with some jock of a phys-ed teacher.

He hadn't wanted to call, feeling the need to see her face when he asked her. So he'd driven out. He himself was surprised at how much it meant to have her go out with him. But he wanted to get her away from the environment of the house, even the town, where they'd grown up. He wanted her to see him as the man he was now. And that he was interested in her as a woman.

That she was pure woman was perfectly discernable at the moment. Her cheeks glowed rosy, her eyes flashed vivid blue, and the swell of her heavy breasts pushed against the cotton of her shirt. She turned from him in agitation, picking up a kitchen towel, and Quent's heart dipped.

"I don't think so, Quent," she said softly.

He just looked at her. She didn't turn around. Well, fine, that was it, then. A man didn't stand around and continue to be rejected.

"Thanks for the cookies and coffee," he said, walking to the door. Keeping his hand deliberately under control, he gently opened the door, stepped outside and closed it behind him.

The bright sunlight hit him as he strode to his truck, and he squinted. Why, he wondered bitterly, wouldn't she go out with him? And why had she acted as though their kiss the other night had never happened? Well, he'd done pretty good in that department, too, he admitted. It had just seemed awkward to bring it up. *But why wouldn't she go out with him?*

He paused, resting his hand on the door handle of his truck. She'd run away from him the other night, and he'd not gone after her to find out why. Now she'd just told him no to a dinner date, and he still didn't know why.

He looked at the house, seeing only Cassie within the kitchen. And he guessed he was going to find out why. Lifting his feet in long determined strides, he walked back toward the house.

He'd asked her out—on a date.

It seemed fantastic, yet she derided herself for that. It had been a simple dinner invitation. Why was she blowing it all out of proportion? Good heavens, he was a man who asked a good many women to dinner.

Like a butterfly above spring pea vines, the memory of his lips upon hers flitted across her mind. How in the world had they ended up playacting with each other as if the kiss of the other night had never happened?

Maybe Quent was as embarrassed and confused by the whole thing as she had been. And it was easier simply to say nothing—what in the world was there to say?

It had happened. The fact sat there. She remembered it vividly. She remembered his very scent.

That he could actually be attracted to her flitted across her mind along with the sure knowledge of his flirting ways with women. But she let those thoughts pass. It didn't matter. Regardless of his intentions, she did not intend to play those games. She didn't intend to play any grown-up games with Quent at all.

The next instant the kitchen door burst inward, blowing all thought into a jumble. Cassie looked up from where she stood, her hands in the dishwater. Quent stood there with a determined glint burning in his eyes.

She just looked at him and blinked. Hadn't he just left? Hadn't she heard his tight-lipped goodbye?

His gaze slid to Q.C. then back to her as he gently shut the door behind him. With catlike grace and an easy air of nonchalance, he walked toward her and leaned against the counter.

For the life of her, Cassie couldn't think of anything to say. The room felt very warm, and her heart beat with uncertainty.

"Don't you think we're both acting a bit foolish?" Quent said, his lips betraying a hint of a smile, though the solid determination of a quest remained apparent.

The situation was totally out of Cassie's control—she felt as though she were buffeted by a wind, uncertain of where to turn, what to do.

"We kissed the other night. And I know you felt something. Are we going to go on like nothing exists between us?" He watched her.

Cassie sighed. "I know." Her voice came softly. "I feel something. I mean, when you look at me—when you touch ... yes, we kissed." She studied him, wonder dawning in her heart. Was he actually saying in a roundabout way that he felt the same fantastic magic? "Do you?" she breathed the question, terrified of asking yet needing to hear the answer.

He understood, grinning broadly beneath his thick mustache.

"Think about that kiss and answer your own question," he said. His expression was answer enough for Cassie. Her pulse throbbed at his sensuous look. The light in his eyes softened. "Cassie, I remember a kiss nine years ago. A kiss from a young woman that has remained in my memory for all that time."

She felt the blood leave her face and looked away. There could be no doubt now. And, Lord, she was so relieved and so frightened, and even so mad, all at the same time. In effect, Quent was proclaiming his interest in her. And she was so very glad—and furious—at herself for that fact. *She wouldn't be happy about it. It could never be. They were not right for each other.*

"What's the problem, Cass? I rather got the impression you liked my kisses." His troubled gaze searched hers.

Cassie gave a shake of her head, looking away. Then she looked back. "You wanted nothing to do with me nine years ago." It was more of a question than a statement.

Quent heaved a sigh. "I was a boy nine years ago. Yes, twenty-one, but still a boy. The thought of what could happen with you scared the pants off me. I certainly couldn't play free and loose with you. And good grief, I felt almost like I'd committed some kind of sin. You were like my own sister."

Looking away, Cassie nodded in understanding. She'd certainly felt all that, too. Touching her chin softly with his fingers, Quent turned her face to his.

"But we're a long way from that time, Cass. And the sky's not blue if I'm mistaken about the attraction between us. What's the problem?"

Looking into his questioning gaze, Cassie searched her heart and mind for an answer. She was attracted to him, powerfully so. And as she looked at him, she saw that Quent had read the knowledge in her eyes. Slowly he lowered his head. Cassie watched his burnished mustache come closer and closer, and then her lids fluttered closed as his warm lips met hers.

The sensation was sweet and drugging, exquisite beyond words. His lips moved upon hers, drawing her to him with their warmth. Then his arms were around her, crushing her against his chest as he moved his hands up and down her back while his rough cheek rubbed hers.

"Cassie," he breathed into her hair, then rained kisses across her temple and down to her neck.

She inhaled his scent, finding it as intoxicating as the feel of his muscles beneath her hands, as his lips upon hers. She couldn't get her breath. Her emotions warred violently. She wanted him to hold her, to caress her, to make her his own, but no, it couldn't be. It could never be. *She could never love him. She wouldn't ever love him. It would kill her, and could even eventually kill him.*

No, she thought vehemently. *No...no.* It was a cry within her soul, a heartrending cry. And then she was saying it out loud, struggling to pull away from his embrace. "No! No!" He was trying to overcome her with his charm—another feminine conquest. Just like her brothers always loved doing. That's all it was.

Pulling away, he looked at her, and his heated expression demanded that she explain.

Fighting to control her breathing, Cassie forced herself to meet his gaze. "I don't want to start something that leads nowhere, Quent," she said firmly, then took a deep breath. She saw the shock in his eyes. "I'm not interested in an affair—in being some good-time girl for a good ole boy."

His pulse throbbed at the hollow of his throat, and his eyes narrowed. "And what makes you think that's what it would turn out to be?"

She cast him a patient look. "I do know you, Quent. Practically as well as I know Mike and Springer." Her look dared him to deny it.

"Okay." Quent nodded, his lips twitching into a grin. "I admit to liking women. But, hey, it's not all one-sided." He grew serious. "We're attracted to each other, Cassie. Don't we owe ourselves the chance to see what it can become?"

"No, we don't," she said more sharply than she had intended. "I don't intend for it to go anywhere. I don't want to be involved with you in any way." She softened her voice. "I have enough with the men of my family."

Quent's gaze rested upon her for a long moment, and she saw him mentally digesting her words.

"You're talking about being a ranger," he said in a low tone.

"That's part of it, Quent. You're just too much like my brothers. And that's not the kind of life I want. Not now. Not ever."

His gold-brown gaze pierced her. "I see," he said coldly. Then he shrugged. "Goodbye, Cass. Thanks again for the afternoon company."

Before she knew it, his callused palm rested against her cheek, and he kissed her fleetingly. He winked. "Just a brotherly kiss."

Then he was gone, and Cassie was left looking at the kitchen door as it closed behind him.

She'd told him the truth and repeated it now to herself. *She'd done the only thing she could, the practical thing, the best thing all around.*

Yes, she'd told him the truth, but there was more to it, her mind whispered accusingly. It wasn't all backed by practical, common-sense thinking. It was backed by fear. She felt self-loathing, hating the fact that she could be manipulated by that fear.

Okay, so fear entered into it, she told herself. It didn't matter. The facts were the same. With the attraction existing between Quent and herself, they were both better off quenching the spark before it became a flame—a flame that could end up leaving both of them charred.

She had no intention of loving a man who spent over half his time away from home, of lying in a cold, empty-feeling bed at night and wondering not only when, but if the man she loved would return.

Q.C. began to whimper, and Cassie picked him up, clutching him to her, her thoughts remaining with the man who could with one kiss turn her blood to liquid fire.

The sun glinted off the hood of the pickup, but the effect was deceptive. The day lay cold beneath a wide blue sky. Quent squinted as he drove the rough road into Doyle City. He'd been out to look at a house, a small one on twenty acres. He was disappointed; the price was high for a house not fit for a horse, much less a man. Even so, he was tempted. He was fast having his fill of living at home.

His thoughts strayed to Cassie, as they invariably had in the past week. He shifted uncomfortably. He didn't need to be thinking about her. She'd made it plain that she wanted nothing to do with him. Her reasons were sound and made good sense. At least they did when he tried to see her side.

The results were the same: she was having nothing to do with him. The thought tightened Quent's chest in anger. It didn't make any damn sense! They were attracted to each other. Man for woman, woman for man sort of thing.

Nearing the school, Quent slowed and maneuvered around several potholes. A movement off the road caught his eye. What at first glance appeared to be a misshapen gray-and-brown boulder turned out on second glance to be human beings—males—one on top of another. They were slugging away, Quent realized. A fight.

Reluctantly deciding against his first impulse to let them go at it, Quent pulled to the side of the road. No friendly scuffle, he saw, but an all-out heated brawl. He'd have to intervene, he supposed: one or both could get hurt. With a long sigh, he opened the door and stretched his legs from the pickup.

Though he called to them, the boys—and Quent used the term loosely, for they were full-grown—didn't hear him approach. They were too engrossed in their fight. There was the thud of fists against bodies, grunts, heavy breathing, jeering threats and cursing.

"Hey," Quent said. "Break it up." He reached for a shoulder, which at that particular moment moved, and bodies tumbled over each other. A foot shot out, tripping Quent, sending him tumbling into the fracas. An elbow sliced into his ribs. Gasping for breath, he let out an oath, cursing not only the boys but himself for clumsiness and for getting involved in the first place.

Regaining his footing, he managed to jerk one of the combatants up by the coat collar, and gave him an angry shake. "I said, that's enough!"

"Let me go!" demanded the boy.

Quent did just that, urging him along with a thrust. For a moment he breathed deeply and watched the boy's retreating back. Then he looked at the other combatant, who was picking himself up from the ground, and was astonished to see that it was Jesse Marlow.

"Jess!" Quent reached for the boy's elbow to help him to stand. He was a tall boy, and almost painfully thin. Dry bits of grass clung to the hair falling into his eyes; blood ran from his nose, and there were several nasty cuts on either cheek. Peering through pain-squeezed eyes, he gave a lopsided grin.

Quent shook his head. "If it's any consolation," he said, "your fighting buddy didn't look so good, either."

"Cassie isn't going to be too happy about the coat." Jesse licked the cut corner of his mouth and shook his coat, indicating the torn pocket. There was a tear in his jeans, as well.

Holding Jesse's chin, Quent surveyed the boy's damaged face. "Come on," he said. "I'll take you to Dad's office and get you cleaned up. You don't want Cassie to see you like this."

At the office, Jesse had yet to say much of anything. He offered several "ouches" as Quent wiped the dried and caking blood from his wounds. Quent couldn't help noticing the boy's resemblance to Cassie. The same sun-blond-colored hair that tended to curl, the same vivid blue eyes.

"You need to pick your sparring partners a little more carefully, Jess," he commented as he reached for another cloth. "This one had about forty pounds on you."

"Uhh," Jesse grunted. "I was doing all right."

Quent hid a smile. "When I was your age, I think we fought over two things—our integrity, of course, couldn't back down when our manhood was challenged, and girls." He cocked an eyebrow. "Which was this one?"

Jesse swallowed, his eyes watering as Quent began with the antiseptic.

"Curt's all hot about Linda," he said. "Thinks I took her away from him. But she's never even dated him, don't want nothin' to do with him." He jutted out his chin. "I guess a woman has a right to date the man she wants."

Quent hid a smile at the terms *woman* and *man*. "Yes," he said, turning his attention to the boy's knuckles. "She does. But I think a man would be more prudent to avoid a knock-down-drag-out over the dispute."

"He was laying for me," Jesse said miserably. Then he straightened. "Besides, a man can't let someone say things about his girl." Conviction laced his voice. "And Curt's been after me for months—he just plain has an ache against me."

"Guess you didn't have much of a choice," Quent said with a nod.

"Cassie's going to be sore." Jesse's battered face took on a hangdog look. "Boy, is she going to be sore. Watch it, will ya," he said, jerking his head away from Quent's ministrations.

"She's just trying to look out for you," Quent said, seeking to steer the conversation around to Cassie. He felt a bit silly and self-conscious about it, but he did it, anyway. "You ought to appreciate the attention she gives you. Before you know it, she'll be married and move out to start a family."

"Cassie?" Jesse shrugged. "Yeah, I guess so."

"This teacher she's been dating," Quent said, appearing to be casually interested, "has she known him long?"

"Yeah, guess so."

"Do they date a lot?"

"Nah," Jesse said.

Carefully Quent taped a small gauze bandage to the wound beneath Jesse's left eye. "Maybe Cassie will take pity on you," he said with a grin.

"Fat chance."

"Does she date anyone else?" Quent asked.

"Who?"

"Cassie."

"Oh—sometimes." Jesse appeared to be thoughtful. "Cassie doesn't date much, though. Guys come around, but they never stay long. She's always got her nose up in the air. And I guess it's because she's too bossy. Know what I mean? She just plain likes to boss men around. Springer says so. And I guess you know."

Quent nodded, again hiding a smile at Jesse's expression and at the pleasing fact Cassie didn't date many men. Then he puzzled over his feelings. Cassie had made her stand plain. He doubted she'd change it. Besides, he didn't want to get serious.

"Maybe the men just don't know how to approach her," Quent offered lightly in a man-to-man fashion. "Do you ever try complimenting her, doing some things for her? She's a woman, even if she is your sister."

"I never thought about it...." Jesse let the words trail off as Quent dabbed ointment on his scraped hand. "Are you interested in Cassie, Quent?"

Jolted by the question, Quent looked up. So much for subtlety, he thought.

"Yes, maybe a little," he admitted with a sheepish slip of a smile.

"I saw you—the other night," Jesse said. His face grew pink. "When you kissed her at the house. Boy, I thought for a minute she was going to smack you good. I almost didn't get off the stairs in time before she come running up." He knotted his brows. "What in the hell was the matter, Quent? She looked madder than a hornet. And you know, she's been touchy ever since." He shook his head. "Women—can't understand them."

"That's the truth," Quent answered fervently. So Cassie has been a bit touchy lately, he mused, ever since that night. He hadn't been so smooth-humored himself, and he knew the cause. He wanted Cassie Marlow. He wanted to touch her creamy skin and feel her warmth. Could it be that Cassie was having the same problem? It was a rhetorical question to which he felt he knew the answer.

Catching his reflection in the mirror over the sink, he realized he was smiling.

When Quent pulled up in front of Marlow Feed and Grain, Jesse's eyes looked none too sure. "She's going to have a fit," he said, his hand on the door handle.

"Hey, I'll face the lioness with you," Quent offered with a grin. Though he was sorry for Jesse's predicament, he was glad for the excuse to see Cassie again.

The figures wouldn't balance. They simply wouldn't balance. With irritation Cassie jerked the tape from the adding machine, crinkled it into a ball and tossed it vengefully into the trash can. Everyone—teachers, efficiency experts, accountants, psychiatrists—they all said if you kept things in order, had a system, there was nothing to maintaining business records. It was common sense; it stood to reason. But it wasn't working!

And where was Jesse? she fumed as she checked the clock. He was more than an hour late. He was supposed to come to the store every day after school, and today she really needed him to help Grover with the inventory in the back. No allowance for two weeks, she thought hotly.

The jingle of the front door sounded, indicating a customer. With a sigh she rose from her desk, her gaze automatically moving to the main aisle, coming to rest on Quent's tall form as he walked forward. Her breath caught; her heart picked up speed. All at once she was foolishly pleased and highly dismayed. He was smiling at her. And he looked so damned handsome.

Then her gaze was drawn to the shorter person beside him. *Good Lord*, she thought, drawing in a shallow breath as the image registered in her brain. *Jesse. He was...he was hurt.*

She felt the blood leave her face; her head whirled slightly. She stood stock-still as the two approached, taking in the cuts and bruises all over Jesse's face, the large bandage high on his left cheek. His coat was torn, and on his jeans—his new jeans—a large tear showed at the knee. He'd been in a fight—again.

Jesse's gaze shifted downward after meeting hers.

"Another fight," Cassie stated flatly. Almost without realizing it, she raised a hand and gingerly touched his face with her fingertips. She looked quizzically at Quent, then back to Jesse. Oh, Lord, his poor face. Her heart constricted. "Oh, Jess, not again." Cold dread slipped down her body, and anger rose in her.

Jesse nodded, his face becoming an insolent mask.

"Who with? Curt Riley again?" she fired off the questions.

"Yeah," Jesse said.

Poor Jesse, she thought as she looked at him, yet she fumed. Fighting. She hated it. And any fool should be able to stay away from fights. And look what it had caused. Here he stood before her, battered and bruised. He could have broken bones. "Anything broken?" she asked anxiously. When he shook his head, she lit into him. "You know better than to fight."

"I didn't start it," Jesse said.

"*I don't care!* You could have finished it by refusing to fight in the first place."

"What was I supposed to do? Run?" Jesse said insolently. Pivoting, he stepped around her. "I'll get to work now."

"Jesse," Cassie called sternly, starting to follow him. "Jesse, I'm talking to you!"

A hand clamped on her arm. "Cassie, leave him be for right now," Quent said.

Cassie whirled around. "I want to talk to him," she said hotly. Looking into his soft brown eyes, she became uncomfortably aware of Quent's nearness. She was shaking, and she immediately averted her gaze. She didn't want to have him view her at this moment, to reveal her emotions in such a way.

"He's all right, Cass," Quent said quietly, seeing clear through to her worry, she realized a bit grudgingly and guardedly. "He's all right, but are you?"

Nodding, she looked up at him. "Thank you for bringing him." She had forced competence into her voice. Uncomfortable under his searching gaze, she moved to her desk and occupied her hands by straightening papers. Quent sauntered behind her and perched himself familiarly on the edge of the desk.

"It's his third fight this school year." Somehow the words just came out. The worry was choking in her throat, bubbling to the surface against her struggle to keep it back. She hadn't talked to anyone, had denied to herself for months that she needed to. "Always with this Curt. The other two fights have been at school. They'll kick him out if it happens again." Quent didn't say anything. Cassie was glad, and felt an odd sense of relief just by having spoken of her worry.

The next instant, before Cassie knew what was happening, Quent slipped from the desk and clamped her hand tight in his own. "You've been working on these books all day, I bet. Time for a break." He tugged at her hand.

"Quent?" She cast him a puzzled look and tried to tug her hand from his. Nevertheless, he started for the door, forcing her to follow him or be dragged along, apparently. "Quent, I can't just leave," she protested, doing what she could to hold back. "I need to finish these books...there's Jesse...Grover...."

"I don't guess the building will crumble to the ground if you take a few minutes off without reporting to a soul." Quent whisked open the door and pulled Cassie out after him.

Despite herself, the spark of enlivening delight rose in her heart. She suddenly felt very much like a caged bird set free. For the moment she was rescued from those stern and unforgiving accounts, from managing the dim and dusty store and from dealing with an unruly brother. And Quent still held her hand.

Yes, become a Silhouette subscriber and the celebration goes on forever.

To begin with, we'll send you:

- 4 new Silhouette Romance novels—FREE
- an elegant, purse-size manicure set—FREE
- and an exciting mystery bonus—FREE

And that's not all! Special extras— Three more reasons to celebrate.

4. Free Home Delivery. That's right! When you subscribe to Silhouette Romance, the excitement, romance and faraway adventures of these novels can be yours for previewing in the convenience of your own home. Here's how it works. Every month, we'll deliver six new books right to your door. If you decide to keep them, they'll be yours for only $1.95 each. And there's **no charge for shipping and handling.**

5. Free Monthly Newsletter. It's the indispensable insider's look at our most popular writers and their up-coming novels. Now you can have a behind-the-scenes look at the fascinating world of Silhouette! It's an added bonus you'll look forward to every month!

6. More Surprise Gifts. Because our home subscribers are our most valued readers, we'll be sending you additional free gifts from time to time—as a token of our appreciation.

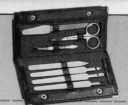

This beautiful manicure set will be a useful and elegant item to carry in your handbag. Its rich burgundy case is a perfect expression of your style and good taste. And it's yours free in this amazing Silhouette celebration!

SILHOUETTE ROMANCE®

FREE OFFER CARD

4 FREE BOOKS

ELEGANT MANICURE SET —FREE

FREE MYSTERY BONUS

PLACE YOUR BALLOON STICKER HERE!

FREE HOME DELIVERY

FREE FACT-FILLED NEWSLETTER

MORE SURPRISE GIFTS THROUGHOUT THE YEAR—FREE

Yes! Please send me my four Silhouette Romance novels **FREE,** along with my manicure set and my **free mystery gift.** Then send me six new Silhouette Romance novels every month and bill me just $1.95 per book, with no extra charges for shipping and handling. If I am not completely satisfied, I may return a shipment and cancel at any time. **The free books, manicure set and mystery gift remain mine to keep.**

CBR017

NAME
(PLEASE PRINT)

ADDRESS   APT.

CITY   STATE

ZIP

Terms and prices subject to change.
Your enrollment is subject to acceptance
by Silhouette Books.

SILHOUETTE "NO RISK GUARANTEE"
- There is no obligation to buy—the free books and gifts remain yours to keep.
- You receive books before they're available in stores.
- You may end your subscription anytime—just let us know.

PRINTED IN U.S.A.

FILL OUT THIS POSTPAID CARD AND MAIL TODAY!

Postage will be paid by addressee

BUSINESS REPLY MAIL
FIRST CLASS   PERMIT NO. 194   CLIFTON, N.J.

SILHOUETTE BOOKS
120 Brighton Road
P.O. Box 5084
Clifton, NJ 07015-9956

NO POSTAGE
NECESSARY
IF MAILED
IN THE
UNITED STATES

Chapter Seven

The abstract euphoria lasted only seconds and was quickly nipped by the crisp north wind.

"Quent, I don't even have my coat," Cassie protested, her implicit common sense returning to nag her back.

But seeming not to hear, Quent firmly pulled her along off the feed store porch and over to his pickup. Catching sight of several avid observers at the gas station across the street, Cassie swiftly and willingly slid into the pickup seat. She groaned inwardly, knowing what rumors would fly, and moved all the way over next to the passenger door as Quent slipped in behind the wheel. He cast her his slow, self-confident grin.

"You won't need your coat in here," he said.

"Just where are we going?"

Quent was backing up the truck. "How 'bout a soft drink at Frosty's." It was a statement, not a question.

Frosty's was a small drive-in restaurant, with three booths inside should one want to eat in amidst the smell of greasy hamburgers and gossipy talk from Opal, the proprietor. Its clapboard sides shone bright white beneath the sun; its hand-painted sign squeaked in the breeze. Frosty's had the thickest, creamiest shakes in the state, in summer or winter.

Quent chose to sit in the truck—anyone with any sense did—and promptly ordered two orange sodas, without asking Cassie's preference. She slid her eyes to him, finding a hint of euphoria slipping again into her veins. Oh, Lord, it was good to have someone take from her shoulders, just for the moment, even such a minute decision as a choice of what to drink. It had simply been one of those days.

She squinted in the sunlight, and worries of Jesse skirted her thoughts. She still had the accounts to do. And here she sat, in close proximity to Quent, extremely aware of his movements, of the fresh earth scent that clung to him, and of his vital maleness. Giving a soft groan, he stretched his long legs. Her gaze moved involuntarily up the length of his legs, jerking away when she reached his trim thighs. She knew he was looking at her and hesitated to look at him.

"So, Jesse's having a bit of trouble?" he asked.

"Yes," she said after a moment, watching the girl bring their drinks out. Time had stopped at Frosty's; the soft drinks were still served in a bottle, complete with a straw.

The young woman smiled alluringly up at Quent as she placed the serving tray on the truck window. "Hi, Quent," she purred. "When am I going to get that helicopter ride?"

"I'll catch you soon," Quent answered smoothly, smiling broadly, giving the young girl a flirtatious wink. He handed her several bills. "Keep the change, and take this tray away."

"Sure, Quent." She spoke his name in a deliberately stretched out and sultry fashion. Her walk back to the restaurant was intended for his view.

Cassie watched the scene in heightening irritation. Oh, she was so familiar with the habit. Just the way it was with her brothers.... Something happened to a female's brains when they got around those men. And they enjoyed it so. Grudgingly Cassie admitted that it was threatening to happen to her too. But, she thought firmly, she'd lived with men like that her whole life. She'd developed a healthy immunity to their charms.

When Quent looked at her, and her hand brushed his as she took her bottle from him, she laughed to herself. She certainly didn't need to be afraid of him. She knew him well. His eyes were warm upon her, and she found herself unloading her worries about Jesse. It seemed perfectly natural.

She told him about the fights at school, of being called in to the principal's office to be told that they would expel Jesse if it happened again on school grounds. Of Jesse's cocky attitude with one teacher. Cassie even confided, "The teacher's a jerk, but Jesse must learn to get along even with the jerks in the world." She could smile then. She told Quent of Jesse's skipping school, of his stubbornness, yet also spoke of his abiding goodness. His grades were respectable, even praiseworthy at times. He did wildly foolish things but never sought to hurt anyone.

Then she found she was even speaking of her worries of her brother's growing sexuality, and her fear that he would get himself into trouble with a young girl. She even mentioned the contents of the note she had found in his pants pocket.

Quent gave a knowing half grin. "And you've talked yourself blue in the face and haven't gotten anywhere."

"You saw today." Cassie sighed. "It was like an explosion between us. I just got so worried, and it came out in anger. It's always like that. I swear it won't be, but I see him retreat behind that wall of defiance, and I . . . I'd like to knock some sense into his blockhead."

"Cassie, all this stuff you've been telling me is just a normal fifteen-year-old boy trying to cope with being on the edge of manhood."

Cassie heard the reassurance in his voice, saw it in his eyes. Somehow, by getting all her thoughts out in the air, they didn't seem so threatening anymore, and she saw the truth in Quent's observation.

As if reading her expression, he grinned. "Think back—remember Mike and me. Remember the time we skipped school and went to the river to target practice with your father's rifle? A rifle we weren't supposed to touch. And what about the time we got into a fight over...what was that girl's name?"

"Tess—April Sewell's sister," Cassie recalled with a wry grin, remembering April's advances to Quent at the party. "It hurt me to see you two fighting."

"Well, fights between us were never lethal. But I had a few that weren't so harmless. Have you talked to Jesse about these fights?" Quent asked.

Cassie looked at him sharply. "I've tried. He clams up. Did he say anything to you? It must be a special conflict of some kind. They've all been with Curt Riley."

"He says it's over his girl—Linda."

Cassie nodded, thinking. "They started about the time he and Linda began dating."

"If you can't talk to him, Cass, get Springer to. And stop worrying. There's nothing wrong with Jesse. He's a normal teenage boy. And a fine one. He'll be okay."

"I know," Cassie sighed. "I truly do. But sometimes I forget. And it's hard to talk to him. I'm the heavy—the one who has to make him bathe and brush his teeth, make him do his homework, eat his spinach. And sometimes I feel that I've done a rotten job. That his problems are all my fault. That he got a bum deal with losing Mom—and then Dad. And he is a Marlow, through and through," she said with a shake of her head. "I don't know."

Quent squeezed her hand. "You sound like a typical mother—and a good one. And Jesse's a good kid with a lot of spunk. It won't hurt him."

"Sometimes I wish he had a bit less 'spunk' as you say."

"Ah, hell. At least he's alive and knows it. And knows how to enjoy life." Quent's eyes sparkled.

A warm feeling of familiarity seemed to envelop Cassie and draw her to him. The light in his eyes grew deeper, hinting at thoughts more intimate, and suddenly Cassie became aware of her hand, still held in his. Her common sense guard flew up, and she tugged her hand away.

"I need to be getting back." Her inner being jangled with conflicting emotions. It had been so good to talk out her worries—and to talk them out with Quent. She felt so...so...no, she didn't! *She would not feel anything around Quentin Hatfield!*

Quent studied her. "Are you afraid of me?" he asked in a low, slow voice.

"Good grief! Of course not." She met his gaze, then looked away, embarrassed, even as she told herself that she refused to be.

"Then why do you keep pulling back? I was trying to be nice—was only holding your hand."

"Oh, you know you were doing more than holding my hand, Quent."

"Anyone could see I was only holding your hand!" Quent protested, on the edge of a chuckle.

"I saw the light in your eyes."

"Oh," he said in a mellow tone. "What did you see, Cass?"

Cassie wished she'd never said anything. Why in the world had she? How in the world did he manage to maneuver her into a position where she revealed more of herself than she ever did to anyone?

"Can we just go?" she spoke tersely. "Jesse can't get home without me, and neither can Cork."

Almost automatically Cassie moved around the kitchen, making dinner. Unseeing, she repeatedly stepped over Cork on the floor and around Springer, who sat in the rocker and watched the evening news on the small portable television. Her mind was elsewhere, wondering at herself, at Quent and at Jesse.

When she turned to set the table, she found plates and silverware already neatly laid out. The surprise jolted her from her thoughts. Looking up, she saw Jesse leaning against the kitchen counter, regarding her.

"Thanks," she said, knowing he'd set the table. The sight of his battered face tugged at her heart. "We're having your favorite—meatloaf."

Jesse nodded, allowing a half grin. Cassie stepped to the oven to check dinner and again her thoughts slipped far away. She recalled the young girl at Frosty's that afternoon and the way she and Quent had smiled at each other. Cassie jerked the dish of meatloaf from the oven, and it thudded as she set it upon a hot pad.

"Let's eat, shall we?" she called out. Both Jesse and Springer gave her funny looks, and Cassie realized she'd spoken unusually loudly and harshly.

Later, comfortable in nightgown and robe, a quilt snug around her shoulders, Cassie sat before the open window in her darkened bedroom. She could hear coyotes yelping not far away. They sounded almost like babies crying.

She thought of little Q.C., and then of Jesse, then of Springer, and all of these thoughts led to Quent.

She squirmed in agitation as his image came sharply before her mind. It wasn't so much a picture of his face as a total sensing of all that made up the man.

The attraction existed; there was no more use in trying to deny the power it held. For the moment she allowed herself to face it, to look at it from all sides, and to savor it. And then fear raised its head.

As if to shut the fear away, and almost before she realized it, Cassie rose and shut the window. With a rapid movement she switched on the bedside lamp. She stood quite still, her gaze roaming the room. It settled on the collage of small pictures on the wall.

She'd always loved taking photographs—oh, not the professional sort, but the true-life action shots she could capture with her Instamatic. Her gaze found the one she sought, the one of Quent holding his trophy after winning the dangerous bull-riding competition at the county rodeo. It was only a three-by-five picture. Lifting it from the wall, she carried it to the light and looked.

He'd been handsome even then; he'd been nineteen, she remembered. Their relationship had been simple: she'd been a troublesome younger sister to him, and he'd been a rambunctious brother. That had been their relationship up until they'd kissed that day at the river. That one wondrous kiss had changed everything. And now....

Cassie sighed. And now they simply couldn't go back. The attraction was there, so strong in her heart that she felt weighed down by it. Did Quent feel the same? She thought of the flirtations of April Sewell and the young woman at Frosty's that day. Perhaps he was no more attracted to her than to any other female. The possibility hurt.

Well, she decided as she jerked down her bed covers, she simply wouldn't think of it. It didn't do any good thinking of it. Vaguely she realized she was being somewhat irrational.

The muffled sound of rock music began. Jesse, no doubt. Frowning, Cassie checked the time, then strode from her room and across the hall. She tapped on his door.

"Jesse?"

"Yeah," came the muffled reply.

Opening the door, Cassie peeked inside. A greenish glow from the stereo faintly illuminated Jesse as he lay in bed, his hands cradling his head. Her first impulse was to snap at him to turn the radio off and go to sleep. She'd even opened her mouth to speak, then shut it.

A bit hesitantly, she stepped into the room. "I can't sleep, either," she said, tiptoeing to his bed. She sat on the edge. He'd removed the bandage from his cheek; the wound looked dark and ugly in the dim light. "You need some aspirin?"

Jesse shook his head.

"Jesse, what is this between you and Curt Riley?"

He shrugged, and Cassie waited, thinking that maybe if she just kept quiet for a minute he'd begin to talk. It worked. After several long seconds Jesse said, "He's just got it in for me, Cass. He has ever since the past summer when our baseball team beat his. Then when I started dating Linda, he added that to his list of grudges.''

''Can't you manage to stay away from him, Jess?''

''I've tried,'' he replied in a plaintive, frustrated tone. ''And what can I do, Cass? I can't run away.''

Cassie nodded. She thought of speaking to him of Linda, of sex, of responsibility, but held her tongue. For once, she admitted honestly, she didn't have all the answers. And this was something she couldn't fix as she'd done with his toy cars or lunch pail when he was younger. Yes, for once sister Cassie was at a loss.

''No, you can't run away,'' she said at last. ''And I'm through asking you to. I'll back you, Jess. If Curt Riley starts anything again, you beat the pants off him.''

She sensed his surprise and thought she saw a half grin. ''I've been trying, Cassie.''

''Well—'' she patted his chest ''—just do the best you can, and try to keep your teeth.'' She started to rise, then stopped. ''You like Linda a lot, Jess?''

''Yeah, I guess so,'' he answered in a guarded tone.

''Jess . . . good night.'' She opened the door.

''Cassie?''

She turned around.

''Quent was asking me about you today,'' Jesse said, then added, ''He's a pretty good guy.''

For a moment she simply stood there. ''Yes,'' she said finally, ''he is a pretty good guy.''

Quietly she returned to her room and snuggled down in bed. What a muddle life could be at times, she thought. What mystery was it that made a person tingle when they saw another person, or made them feel nothing at all? It didn't seem to have rhyme or reason. It certainly didn't matter whether or not it was practical or beneficial.

If she gave in to her attraction to Quent, if she went to dinner with him, saw him just a little, what harm would it do? It certainly didn't mean they were on the edge of an impassioned love affair and heading down the aisle, to marriage, for goodness' sake.

And yet fear nipped at her. It was fear of the unknown, in herself, in Quent, in the situation. What if it did get out of hand? What if she ended up brokenhearted? What if she fell for Quent only to lose him to the harsh vulgarities that life could bring? And with a man like Quent, the odds were not in her favor.

She slept fitfully, dreaming of Quent's lips upon hers and the sound of his mellow voice cajoling, teasing.

She woke to Jesse calling her. "Hey, sleeping beauty. Time to rise and shine." Jesse was bending over her, shaking her shoulder.

It took her several seconds to focus, several surprised seconds. Jesse never rose before her; it was always the other way around.

"I'll bring you up a cup of coffee," he tossed to her along with a grin as he left her bedroom.

"Thanks," Cassie managed. There was a closeness between them. What a miracle simply listening to him had wrought, she thought. The image of his bruised face lingered in her mind as she slipped into her robe. Things couldn't continue as they had, she decided. She debated her plan for a moment—force was rarely, if ever, an answer to anything. Yet, in this case, there was little else left. And sometimes you had to fight fire with fire. With purposeful strides she walked down the hall to Springer's room.

Springer listened to her relate the problem Jesse was having with Curt Riley, his expression growing darker by the moment. "So I want you to threaten this kid, Springer," Cassie said firmly. "And make it good so he won't go saying anything about Jesse not fighting his own battles. I don't want Jesse to ever know we did this."

The whole idea surprised her. It wasn't her way to think of something like this, something bordering on being crude and devious. But something had to be done. Jesse was her brother, and she would not stand by and allow some bully to keep hurting him.

"I'll take care of it, Cass," Springer said. "There won't be any more trouble."

Looking at her giant of a brother, Cassie had to smile. Curt Riley would have no way of knowing that within Springer's huge body really lived a pussycat. But then, when Jesse was threatened, she supposed Springer turned out just like herself, a very irritated and protective tiger.

"Hey, Cass," Springer said as she turned to go. "I'll talk to Jesse like you wanted me to. Guess it couldn't hurt to go over the facts of life." He chuckled. "Maybe Jess'll teach me something."

"Thanks, Springer." She cast him a grateful smile.

Well, she thought as she gave a long sigh, that was one big worry off her mind. Now there was still the store's accounts to deal with—and her feelings for Quent. She cringed at the last thought, and Quent's name echoed within her. He was not a problem at all, she told herself firmly. He simply wasn't. What a silly idea. Finding the picture of him that she'd taken from the wall, Cassie stalked over and hung it with a firm hand. She didn't look at it.

As she dressed for the day, she sipped the coffee Jesse had brought her, smiling now and again. She'd better enjoy that cup of coffee. Jesse may never be so thoughtful again. Deliberately she kept her mind on things needing to be done at the store, on the shopping she'd promised to do for Lettie, and the tentative lunch date she'd made with Anita. On a last minute impulse, she took time to put on a bit of makeup. She was quite pleased with her reflection in the mirror.

Gliding down the stairs, she gave in to a tuneful hum. It was sunny again; a day made to lift spirits.

"Hello, everyone," she called as she pushed through the kitchen door. The next instant she almost dropped the now-empty coffee cup as her gaze fell immediately to Quent, sitting in a straight line from the door.

Smiling at her, he drawled a mellow "Good morning, Cass." She read the knowledge in his eyes. He knew he'd surprised her; his eyes twinkled with . . . Cassie wasn't quite sure with what. But it unnerved her. She felt the attraction as she never had before.

It was early morning, and no one, Quent thought, should have the thoughts he was having at this time of the morning. He allowed his eyes to flick over Cassie in a friendly manner, but even with that quick glance he took in the womanly shape beneath her soft shirt and slim-fitting jeans. Sipping his coffee, pretending to watch the morning news with Springer, he glanced at her again as she walked across the wide kitchen; her heavy breasts swayed. She had a smooth way of walking that drew a man's eyes.

When her gaze had met his, Quent was sure of the attraction between them. But now he wondered if it had simply been a figment of his imagination, perhaps because he wanted it to be there. Why he wanted it to be there, he wasn't quite sure. Not that it worried him, except that he was having trouble figuring out exactly how he felt about Cassie. She attracted him, that he knew, but he was wondering to what depth. He had a growing suspicion that he was more interested in Cassie than he had ever been in any woman in his life.

When Springer had asked him out for breakfast so that they could get an early start driving down to the southern part of the state for the day, Quent had readily agreed.

Cassie was her calm, orderly self, helping Lettie get breakfast on the table and joining in the casual talk. If her eyes were drawn to him, as his were to her, Quent didn't see it. He wondered if she was deliberately avoiding looking at him. At least that possibility gave him hope of her interest, an interest that he was so sure was there one minute and so doubtful of the next.

"Oh, Quent," Springer said as he lavishly ladled gravy over his biscuits, "I almost forgot to tell you. I heard yesterday that the Snowden place is for sale. It's that house just over the rise down the road, next to our property. It looks to need some work—I haven't looked at it in years—but there's near a quarter section goes with it."

"I don't really need that much land," Quent said.

Cassie looked up then, straight into his eyes. "Are you looking for a house, Quent?" Her eyes were incredibly blue. The air seemed to vibrate between them, and there was no doubt in Quent's mind that she felt it, too.

"Yes," he answered, his thoughts on other things as he looked into those shimmering eyes. "I'm used to living on my own."

"Nobody needs that much land anymore, Quent," Springer was saying, "unless you want a small place to farm on the side. And there aren't too many people wanting to get into that work anymore. But you can enjoy it. And the price may be good. I don't know what Snowden is asking, but he's moved down to Texas now. He may want to get it off his hands."

Cassie looked away, busying herself with refilling everyone's coffee cups, and Lettie was repeating some old gossip about Snowden. Jesse joined in with a wild rumor he'd heard.

"Who do I see about the place?" Quent asked Springer. He remembered the section of land from childhood, rolling hills, fair amount of tall timber, good proximity to town. And the fact that it was close to the Marlow place played at the edges of his mind.

He and Springer left right after breakfast. He felt let down but didn't know what he'd expected. He'd just been drawn to coming out and seeing Cassie, to being in the house with her.

He didn't fully understand himself and his emotions. They seemed to be growing and changing so fast. It used to be easy when he'd had these feelings for a woman: he would romance her and make love to her and enjoy all the relationship had to bring until it would fade of its own accord.

But this time was different. For one thing, Cassie was having nothing to do with him. For every step he took toward her, she backed up two. He'd never had a time when a woman rejected him. Well, he conceded reluctantly, maybe once or twice in his lifetime, so long ago that he couldn't remember.

He'd never felt this strongly for a woman, experiencing an attraction so powerful that he went to sleep thinking of her and awoke with her soft image lingering from misty dreams.

Perhaps his time had finally come, the time of finding the one woman. It wasn't the first time he'd had the thought. It unnerved him, the very idea being foreign and unknown. A man never knew what kind of husband he'd make, what kind of father. The responsibility was enough to make a man ride hard and fast in the opposite direction. *Yet*, he thought in frustration, *how was he ever going to find out if Cassie wouldn't give him a chance?*

Chapter Eight

As a man is drawn to a cheery fire on a cold winter's night, Quent was drawn by the dim light shining from the Marlow Feed and Grain store. Not that he hadn't known that Cassie was there; Springer had told him she'd returned to work on the accounts at the store, where she was assured of peace and quiet. Personally Quent thought that Springer should have been more prudent than to let her stay down at the store alone at night. Life in the country wasn't as secure as it had been ten or twenty years ago.

Apparently Cassie, engrossed in her paperwork, hadn't heard his truck or seen its lights. Peering through the door window, Quent saw her head bent over the desk. Two bright lamps illuminated the desk area in the otherwise dark store.

He gently turned the knob; the bell above the door jingled as he entered. Cassie's head shot up. Surprise registered across her features, then she smiled, a radiant, warm, welcoming smile. Magnetic energy filled the air between them even at this distance. It was brief, but there for sure, Quent told himself as she quickly replaced the naturally warm smile with one of wary caution.

"Springer told me you were here," he said as he walked toward her desk. "I thought maybe you could use some help."

And he thought that perhaps if he spent some time with her, undemanding, not pushing, not daring even to touch her, she'd let down her guard. Maybe he could melt her reserve. For he'd come to a conclusion, a very awesome conclusion: *he was falling in love with Cassie Marlow.*

Cassie's first thought was, Why? But she didn't say it. It seemed rather a rude question to put to someone who'd just extended a friendly helping hand, and maybe she didn't truly want to know the reason.

"It's really a one-person job," she said, her gaze flickering away from Quent's, moving down his wide chest. Nervously it flicked back up to settle on his hair. "It's time consuming, more than anything else."

She felt his gaze as a soft caress. With pantherlike steps, he rounded the desk and stood close behind her. She caught the mingling scents of musky after-shave and cool night dew. She was so aware of him that she sensed his heartbeat. Her own thudded loudly. Surely he could hear, she thought. She wished he'd leave yet hated the prospect, all at the same time.

"Oh, surely there's something I can do." He peered closer. "Out of balance?" He picked up the machine tape. "I'll call out the figures to you. You'll go blind trying to check them yourself." With that he pulled a chair to the edge of the desk, then looked at Cassie expectantly. His soft brown eyes glowed with warm, friendly light.

A sparkle of something undefinable hit her heart, not to be extinguished, though she quickly averted her gaze to the ledger book.

With his calling out the figures she quickly found her mistakes. Then, while she continued on with the ledgers, he checked invoices for double billing and back orders. Quent began to joke with her, forcing her to smile and to talk to him. They compared notes on Q.C.'s growth and spoke of "times when" from their childhood. Gradually Cassie relaxed. She was somewhat surprised when she closed the last ledger and realized they'd completed the work she'd expected to take her the whole week.

"Last of it," Quent commented as he poured two cups of coffee, emptying the glass pot. He set a cup on the desk in front of Cassie.

"Thanks." She stretched her arms. "I can hardly believe we did all that."

"Well, lady, it's nearing eleven o'clock." Quent grinned above his coffee cup.

"It is?" Unbelieving, she glanced quickly to the clock. "It is," she repeated flatly, with a shake of her head. The time had flown, and she admitted as she looked at Quent that she'd enjoyed it.

As Cassie locked the store's door, Quent stood very close. She fancied she could feel his breath. Every fiber of her body seemed attuned to him, waiting. He accompanied her to her truck, walking close enough for his arm to brush hers. They each made idle comments about the sidewalks being rolled up and winter finally hitting hard; their breath steamed in the cold air. When Quent raised a hand to open the pickup door for her, she started slightly.

"Good night," he said just before closing the door after her. He gave a parting wave.

Cassie started for home, watching Quent in the rearview mirror drive away in the opposite direction.

He hadn't kissed her. He hadn't even tried. He hadn't made any kind of advance at all.

That fact sat heavily on her heart, as well as the confusing knowledge that she very much wished he had. Her entire body longed for him; it was almost an actual physical ache.

No, she thought, she shouldn't find longing after him confusing. It was as old as the human race. It was the longing of a woman for a man she not only was attracted to, but cared for. There—it was out. Admitted to her heart. She cared for Quent. She always had, and now it was deepening. What was she going to do about it?

When Cassie came into the kitchen, she found a note from Springer. He'd been called out. "Don't worry," he'd written above his name.

Immediately pain squeezed Cassie's heart. Oh, Lord, she didn't want to feel this way, this rush of her pulse, fear welling up in her throat. *Would it never stop?* Firmly she pushed the thoughts of fear down.

Down, but not out, she knew. As she undressed and made ready for bed, the mental pictures of Springer turned into images of Quent. The visions were shadowed in her mind, her imagination picturing fleeting and distorted catastrophes. As fast as she pushed the dreaded thoughts away, others took their place. It was always this way, Cassie battling for control, knowing her visions of disaster were not only irrational but harmful. Yes, knowing, but fighting a never-ending battle to persuade her inner self.

There was no getting around the fact that one night her father had gone out on patrol, and she'd never seen him alive again. Yes, it had scarred her. She tried to rise above it, but it was rough going.

Longing to feel Quent beside her, his secure arms around her, and listening for Springer's steps on the stairs, Cassie tossed and turned, falling asleep only to jar awake and listen to the quiet house. Finally, near five o'clock, Springer's truck sounded in the yard. Cassie fell asleep before she could hear him come up the stairs.

The next day Springer dismissed his work of the night before as the routine routing of some rowdies. Deer season had just opened, and some hunters who'd been camping at the edge of the river had gotten a little exuberant, no doubt helped along by too much spirits, and were having target practice at a farmer's barn. The farmer's house, which happened to be nearby, took a few stray shots.

Listening to Springer relating the incident the next evening, Cassie sensed something that she couldn't name. It was in the tone of his voice; he sounded almost deliberately casual. He let the subject drop, however, and she pushed her unease aside. It was always like this. *He's home*, she thought. *He's home and safe.* Firmly she forced the plague of dread from her mind. There was too much to do to put up with foolish shadows chasing her thoughts. It was almost Thanksgiving. Everywhere she turned she was bombarded with reminders of the coming holiday season, her very favorite time of year.

On Thanksgiving Day Cassie was lying on the couch in the living room, feeling full and groggy. Sunlight shining through the window warmed her. She proudly felt she'd outdone herself with dinner this year. Of course, Springer'd had a hand in it. The turkey he'd shot had been a prize. There was disappointment in Mike's not coming home for the holiday; he'd remained in Denver, hinting at a special girlfriend he didn't want to leave. There had been a void at the table, and it wasn't just Mike's absence. Cassie realized she missed Quent. It seemed as though he should be there with them—with her.

In the past week he'd seemed to appear every time she turned around. He had had dinner at the Marlow home, dropped in at Anita's while Cassie visited, and one day ran into her at the grocery store. "Picking up a few things for Mom," he'd told her, flashing his mellow grin. He'd pushed his cart alongside Cassie's throughout the entire store. She'd begun to look forward to their accidental meetings.

Now, while she lay there, half dozing and savoring the warm sunlight, she heard a strange sound. She listened, trying to decide what it was. It grew louder and became distinguishable as a helicopter. Quent's helicopter, Cassie realized, hovering right over their house!

In an instant she was up and running to the kitchen. Through the window she spied the giant glass-and-steel bird setting down in the backyard. Springer and Jesse were already walking to meet Quent.

Cassie hesitated on the porch, looking at him. The sun shone golden on his brown hair. As if sensing her presence, he looked beyond Springer to the house. Their gazes caught and held. As though drawn by a powerful magnet, she stepped from the porch and walked toward him, her eyes never wavering from his face. Something within her quivered, in fear, in anticipation, for she knew instinctively that today was going to be different. Today she'd have to step beyond the wall of protection she'd built around herself—*or step forever back*.

He held his hand out to her. She was aware of Springer and Jesse turning to look at her, felt their curiosity, but didn't remove her gaze from Quent's.

"How about a ride?" he asked.

She looked uncertainly at him, then slid her gaze to the helicopter. She didn't know if she wanted to take any step at all. Her hand was warm in his. He waited.

"Yes." She nodded, her mouth slipping into a smile.

An eager smile swept Quent's face. In quick motion, he opened the door for her. "We'll be back before dark," he tossed to Springer as he helped Cassie step up into the mechanical bird. Jesse hollered something about a coat, tearing off his and pressing it into her arms. Quent slammed the door securely.

Her seat rocked as he jumped into the one beside her. His hands brushed her shoulder as he helped her on with Jesse's coat. Their eyes met. Quickly, as if fearful of causing her to change her mind, Quent looked away.

Cassie squinted in the brightness, and Quent handed her a pair of dark sunglasses. The engine growled to life. The blade swung above, swooping through the air faster and faster. She looked at her brothers; they stood near the house, the wind whipping bits of winter-dead grass around them and tearing at their hair. Jesse gave a half wave; Springer looked to be scowling.

Her heart dipped as the machine lifted and the ground receded. They were flying up into the beautiful blue sky. Quent moved a lever, and they zoomed above the trees. Cassie marveled. She hadn't realized a helicopter could move so fast. He flew up and glided down, turned and momentarily Cassie could look sideways at the ground. She saw the Wichita Mountains shrouded in haze, then Quent turned the machine and followed the river.

She saw him peering down, seeming to look for something. He dropped the machine lower and shot Cassie a questioning glance. She smiled her pleasure; he smiled back. Once more his attention was drawn to the ground. He moved the helicopter above the trees then over the road, passing over a tractor-trailer truck, then heading back for the river.

Flying straight toward a rocky butte jutting from the bend in the river, he smoothly set the helicopter down upon its top and cut the engine.

"Come on," he said, reaching for a pair of binoculars. "I want to show you something."

Rounding the helicopter, he caught her by the waist and swung her down. Even through the thickness of her coat, she tingled at the touch. With every beat of her heart she felt herself moving ever closer to Quent. Taking her hand, he pulled her to the crest of the butte; the river flowed below, west to east. The wind whipped around her, and the bright sun caused her to squint.

"The world at our feet," Cassie breathed as she took in the vast panorama displayed before them.

Quent smiled in understanding but didn't allow her to remain still to look. Pulling her to the edge, he led her down what very loosely could be called a path. His hand squeezed hers as he guided her steps. She looked down once, then kept her attention on the ground before her.

With surprise, she saw a ledge appear before them and a minute later found herself standing beside Quent on a wide shelf. Sheltered completely by rock and earth on three sides, it faced south, was bathed in sunlight and snuggly warm.

Using the binoculars, Quent searched another smaller butte across the river and to the west. "There." He pointed and handed the binoculars to her. "Look near the bottom by that cedar." His hand settled at the base of her neck, beneath her coat collar. His thigh brushed hers.

Peering through the glasses, Cassie searched the side of the butte. Then she saw them: three golden bobcat cubs playing among the rocks. A larger cat, their mother, she guessed, lay atop a rock enjoying the sun.

Cassie's heart warmed with pleasure at the sight. "When did you find them? Oh, there's another!" she cried before Quent could answer as the little fellow tumbled from some dry grass.

"There should be four babies and their mother," Quent said. "Found them about three weeks ago. The mother was injured in some way. I couldn't get close enough to find out how, not without disturbing them to a great extent."

"What did you do?" Cassie asked, still enjoying watching the small cats' antics.

"I dropped meat from the chopper. It gave her and the babies enough for her to heal on her own."

"How clever!" Cassie laughed in her delight, turning her gaze to his. "Is she all right now?"

Quent nodded, taking the binoculars from her hand and having another look. "Seems to be. I stopped feeding her a week ago. She waits for her free meal once in a while, though."

"Have you been coming every day?"

"Pretty much."

"I wonder how long it will be until someone finds them," Cassie said, sadness lacing her voice. She knew many people enjoyed killing them just for the gratification of killing animals.

"Oh, they'll be safe for a few months. Until they're old enough to start roaming away from the butte."

He swung the glasses away from the cats and appeared to study something more to the south. Gradually he fanned the glasses toward the river.

"What is it?" Cassie asked, sensing that his interest was more than casual.

But Quent shrugged and gave her an easy grin. "Just looking."

He moved to sit, leaning against the flat face of rock. Cassie sat beside him. The rocks had absorbed heat from the sun and gave it back again. A hawk flew near, then veered away as it spotted the cliff's human occupants.

Looking straight ahead, all that they could see was crystal blue sky. It was almost as if they'd escaped the earth to an isolated haven of their own, completely unreachable.

"You come here often, don't you?" she asked quietly, not looking at him. She sensed that he nodded.

"Often as I can." He gave a small chuckle. "And I can't be accused of loafing on the job. I can see the whole county south from here. Up above, I can see north, too."

She felt him look at her as his voice trailed away. Cassie's heart thudded. The side of her body nearest him seemed to tingle. She marveled at the sensations. She knew he'd brought her up to the isolated butte for a very special reason, and she couldn't sort out how she felt about it, or what would be the best thing to do about it. She knew she shouldn't have come, but she wasn't sorry. She wanted to be with him like this. Lord help her. She knew she was making a mistake but simply didn't want to reason with it anymore.

She didn't turn her head even as she sensed him leaning toward her. Gently he placed his fingers to her chin and turned her head toward him. She lifted her gaze to meet his, and it was as if a surge of electricity flowed from him into her, shattering, very slowly, bit by bit, any fragment of reserve left within her.

His eyes studied her, questioning. She saw doubt flicker there, then growing heat. She touched his cheek, moving her fingertips to his mustache; the hairs were thick, painted almost red by the sun. As though of their own volition, her eyes closed, and her lips parted.

His kiss came, tender as the morning, deep as the darkest night. Briefly he drew back, cupping her face in his callused hands, then brought her lips again to his. All Cassie could think of were those lips, warm, growing heated upon her own, then his mouth opening to her, taking from her.

Moving to his knees, Quent pulled her hard against his chest. His strong arms supported her. And she kissed him, wrapping her arms around his neck when he seemed to be about to pull away.

Breathless, they broke away from each other. Cassie clung to him, her heart throbbing. His cheek was pressed roughly to hers, and then his lips seared a trail to the tender side of her neck. Vaguely Cassie heard him murmur, "Cassie... Cass..." Then he let out something that was a near-growl and tugged impatiently at her oversize coat. It slipped from her shoulders, and dimly Cassie realized that Quent removed his, too. Then he was laying her back. The softness of sheepskin brushed her cheek. She was warm, pulsing with warmth. Quent's face floated above hers, his head framed by a halo of bright sunlight.

Cassie raised her arms to him, murmuring his name, gathering him to her as he pressed his body along the length of hers. His kiss was hard, demanding, and she answered in kind, hungrily running her hands through his thick hair.

It was alluring magic, such as she'd never felt before. Heat, vibrant and insistent, pulsed through every part of her body. Quent's cheek was rough against hers, his hair like a rich bobcat pelt in her hands. His shoulder and back muscles were rock hard beneath the softness of his flannel shirt; the skin at his neck was as sleek as velvet. His hand moved hesitantly over her breasts, and instinctively Cassie arched to meet his touch.

With every heartbeat her desire grew. This was what it was like to love a man. Quent. Her heart sang his name. He held her. It was his lips caressing her skin, his strong hands molding her body, that caused her spirit to soar on the wings of wonder and pleasure.

A whisper of warning crossed her spinning mind. *No... no...* she denied the whisper that sought to draw her back. It all felt too wonderfully exquisite—with the promise of so much more. She didn't want to lose the moment; she wanted to follow the passions that were sweeping her onward.

Quent's hand moved upon the skin of her abdomen. His palm was work-roughened, but the sensation he caused with his strokes was so sweet.

No...no... she tried denying again the insistent whisper of warning.

Cassie's body answered his every touch; she was warm, so warm. Quent reveled in the feel and scent of her as he nuzzled the sultry valley between her full breasts and kissed the delicate skin that rose above the lace of her bra. His mind repeatedly called her name, as if to draw her completely to him. He wanted her desperately, all of her, as he never had any other woman in his life.

He knew he was losing control and made an attempt to grasp for reason, even as he covered Cassie's legs with his, pinning her beneath him. But the burning need within swept him on. Impatiently his hand fumbled with her blouse as he sought complete access to her skin, her warm, satiny skin.

Then he realized she'd stilled beneath him. She trembled and pushed at his chest, though with a weak effort. Slowly, trying to clear his brain from the fog of passion, Quent raised himself on one elbow and looked down at her. She was trembling—or was it himself who was shaking? She'd turned her face from him.

"Cassie?" His palm against her cheek, he drew her head toward him. Her lashes were long and dark against her cheeks; he saw tears escape beneath them. "Cassie?" he asked again, dismayed confusion tugging at him. What was wrong? He shouldn't have let it go this far, but, hell, they both were still fully clothed. No, it wasn't that—what was it?

She opened her eyes then closed them again. "I..." She dropped her head to the crook of his arm. "I've never felt this before. I didn't know—and we really shouldn't—I'm just not ready. Not sure." She whispered the words in a barely coherent fashion.

A cold chill of astonishment swept over Quent. He understood she was telling him that she wasn't ready to make love to him, but adding her words to his instinct, he suspected something more.

"Cassie," he asked in a low voice, "are you saying you've never made love to a man?"

She pushed at him, sliding up into a sitting position, and seemed to realize for the first time that her blouse was unbuttoned. To Quent's amusement, pink splotches appeared on her cheeks. Still avoiding his gaze, she pulled her blouse together and began buttoning it. Quent just waited, staring at her, impelling her to answer.

She shook her head. "No." Her voice was barely audible.

"No what?" Quent persisted. "No, you haven't made love to a man, or no, that's not what you're saying."

"I haven't." She flashed him a fleeting glance before returning her attention to buttoning her blouse.

"But you're twenty-seven years old," Quent protested, unbelieving.

Cassie's head jerked up, and her eyes were wide. "Is that some sort of sexual license? Have I broken some law? I guess I can decide how I want to live, what's right for me. And I have had plenty of chances." She jutted out her chin in a haughty fashion. "I do know what it's all about."

Quent stared at her defiant face, her jutting chin, which trembled slightly. The truth of the matter hit him like an exploding star, swelling not only his heart, but his male ego. Cassie had never yielded to another man. But she had been ready to for him. He knew that. Even now, all he had to do was reach out and touch her. He saw it in the shimmering longing in her eyes, felt it in the warmth that vibrated between them.

When Quent reached for her, Cassie couldn't keep from going into his embrace. He sat back against the warm rock and nestled her into his shoulder. His thumb caressed her neck, sending shivers of delight down her spine. His breath fanned her temple.

She was not alone in her trembling. Time clicked slowly by as she tried to quiet her body, though every heartbeat seemed to battle against her. She wanted Quent. Her mind refused to let go of the sweet memory of only minutes before. What did it matter that their love might not be true and that she simply couldn't risk falling in love with him? For him—well, he'd made love to women before and would no doubt forget it. And for her, she'd have this time. This one time with him. She could force herself to face the truth later. They were here now—and she did love him so.

She nuzzled his neck, inhaling his alluring male scent. Almost without realizing it, she moved her fingers between the buttons of his shirt, seeking his smooth skin. He groaned, and then his lips were on hers, harsh and demanding, giving and taking passion, and again she was spinning away into that wondrous realm of sensations.

With a violent motion Quent tore his lips away and pressed her head against his chest, holding her tightly against him. Resisting, she trailed her lips along his neck. *She wanted him so.*

Quent shuddered. "No, Cassie," he whispered, rocking her slightly. "Not like this. I can't. Not like this."

She clung to him, her body aching, her mind in wild confusion. Did he no longer want her because he'd found out her inexperience? The possibility tore at her pride.

Minutes later his embrace loosened, and she looked up into his face. It was drawn with strain. She knew that, for whatever reasons, he was fighting his desires, as well. *Oh, Quent,* she thought, *I want you.* And she couldn't bear to see the pain on his face. Her heart lifted when he smiled.

"You're beautiful," he breathed.

Maybe, just maybe, Cassie allowed, he was in love with her. Truly in love. And yet a shadow fell across her spirit. *Did it matter? They still weren't right for each other.* It would be a disaster. Every time he left her, she'd wonder if he was coming back. Piece by piece, she knew she'd die, just as her mother had. And sooner or later, like her father, Quent would resent her, for she wouldn't be able to keep the fear to herself.

Or could she?

He touched her hair. "Let it loose," he said.

She reached up to remove the clip that bound her long hair. Taking it in his hands, he pulled it forward, fanning it through his fingers and allowing it to fall over her shoulders and across her breasts. He looked at it, and then at her as if he were viewing something precious. Cassie's heart thudded.

"Before, when you said you weren't ready. That you weren't sure," he said, watching her closely. "Does that mean you think you may be in love with me?"

With a shake of her head Cassie looked away, searching her heart and mind for an answer.

"I'm in love with you, Cassie. I think I have been for a long time."

Slowly she turned back to face him. She read the truth in his words. Joy and fear battled within her. He was waiting for her to say something. Frantically she tried to sort out what she could say and still keep a part of herself hidden.

"I think I love you, too," she said. "But that doesn't mean we're right for each other, Quent."

Chapter Nine

"That's true," Quent said slowly. His eyes darkened as they studied her. Giving a beguiling smile, he took her hand. "But don't you think we should have the chance to find out?"

He made perfect sense, Cassie thought as the warmth of his eyes caressed her. She adored those eyes. She tried not to, knowing full well the dangers there, but they evoked feelings within her that she never dreamed could be. A shadow touched her thoughts, reminding her of the fear. She denied it, pushed it away. She'd hidden and dealt with it for this long.

"Yes," she said, her gaze captured by his. The longing throbbed through her body, tantalizing her beyond better judgment.

Quent's smile broadened. As if reading her thoughts, he gave a reluctant shake of his head. "I didn't mean in that way. I think we'd both better be sure of where we're headed before getting carried away in that vein."

"Why?" Cassie asked plainly.

"Your brothers, for one thing. They'd all be after me if I played fast and loose with their sister."

"My brothers have never interfered in my love life; I don't make it a habit to tell them about it." She felt her control returning and with it the power to tease him for what seemed to her his total male inconsistencies.

"Springer's last words to me before we took off this afternoon were 'She's my sister.'"

Cassie opened her mouth in surprise. "He didn't."

"He did." Quent smiled at her expression.

"It doesn't matter," Cassie said with a toss of her head. "Don't tell me none of the women you've made love to had brothers."

"None as big as yours," Quent teased.

It rankled that he didn't deny his many amorous experiences. Oh, he was so like her brothers. The thought stabbed her as the comparison came sharply to mind. She'd been lured away by her emotions and had forgotten the truth of the situation. Mentally seeking to draw within herself, she moved as if to rise.

Quent reached for her, gently grasping the handiest hold: her hair. He looked into her eyes, then loosened his grip and stroked her hair, sending vibrations quivering through her body. The hard fight for common sense began to slip.

But Quent said, "This is serious, Cassie. I'm serious. I'm not playing around."

Studying his eyes, Cassie saw the earnestness there. He took her into the crook of his arm. She went willingly, even as she criticized herself. It just felt too good to resist. They gazed out at the earth beyond the lofty summit. She felt his heartbeat against her side, and her heart quivered with delight, with wonder, and with a myriad of doubts.

As the sun fell lower in the sky, they talked. Quent spoke to Cassie of the things he'd seen and done, the things he still wanted to do. At first it was like talking to a brick wall; she was withdrawn, even seeming not to hear, only the occasional twitch of her eyes betraying that she did.

But he persisted. He told her of his idea of beginning a Christmas tree farm and found she knew quite a lot about the subject and had been interested in the idea, as well. At least he had finally hit upon a subject that got her talking to him.

He saw the romantic, womanly side of Cassie that he'd not been perceptive enough to see when they were kids growing up together. She liked the music of Don Williams and Eddie Rabbit, enjoyed old movies, Jimmy Stewart ones especially, and her favorite color was brown.

"Brown?" Quent asked, puzzled. "No one's favorite color is brown."

"Mine is—it's the color of the earth," she said.

Quent nodded in agreement, enjoying watching her eyes. They were a vivid crystal-clear blue, seeming to have endless depth. And, he noticed curiously, they were wary, too. Not always, only now and again would he see caution slip into them. She didn't betray it on her face, only in her eyes.

Occasionally his gaze slipped to her breasts. If she noticed, she didn't reveal it. And, Quent told himself, he wouldn't be male if he didn't look at that part of her anatomy. With a wry inward grimace, he reminded himself of his vow to keep his hands off. He would wait, wait until she was sure of her feelings for him. Then she'd give all of herself to him, not just a hesitant part, a part that afterward would cause her to regret, and taint what they did with shame.

He wanted all of Cassie, and he wanted it to be good between them.

The sun was just falling below the horizon when he set the chopper down in the Marlow backyard. Springer stood on the porch and watched them approach. His narrow gaze surveyed Cassie closely, then slipped to Quent.

Cassie must have sensed her brother's reserve, but she only said "It was a wonderful ride," and smiled.

"I won't stay," Quent murmured, tugging Cassie to him. Since Springer stood on guard, he only brushed her forehead with a light kiss. She pulled away quickly, casting an uncertain glance from him to her brother.

"Good night," she said to Quent. The caution flickered in her eyes, then her smile changed from being hesitant to warm, before she left him and Springer alone. Quent watched the soft sway of her womanly rounded bottom, musing that she gave faded denims a new dimension.

"That's my sister you're looking at." Springer was leaning against his house, his hands pushed into his pockets. Being up on the porch put him several feet above Quent who stood at ground level—and Springer's immense height added to that effect.

"I know that," Quent answered easily. He waited for the big man to speak his piece.

"I guess I can't ask what went on with you two this afternoon," Springer said bluntly. "I know your way with women." He let that sit there a moment. "But this is Cassie. Are you serious about her?"

Quent hid a smile at the unfamiliar role Springer had assumed. Yet he was proud of him and would have been critical of anything less.

"Yes," Quent said, his eyes not wavering, giving his younger friend the respect that was due.

With a big sigh, Springer stepped from the porch and extended an arm to Quent. As they shook hands, he said, "I hope to hell you know what you're getting into, but if anyone can finally handle Cassie, it'll be you."

"Now can you really see anyone actually trying to handle Cassie?" Quent quipped.

Springer nodded grudgingly.

"Springer," Quent said, almost reluctant to speak, yet wondering. "Is there something I should know about Cassie? I mean, has anything happened to her in the years since I've been gone?" He didn't truly know what he meant, so he couldn't put it into words. It came out as a nonsensical question.

Springer frowned in puzzlement. "Dad died, if that's the type of something you mean. Why? What's wrong?"

"Nothing, I guess," he tossed off with a shrug. "Just sometimes I have the feeling something is eating at her.

She. . . ." Watching a wide grin slip over Springer's face, he broke off.

"She isn't the same girl-next-door you knew, buddy." Springer slapped him on the back. "That's for sure. You're seeing her as a woman—and you're simply having doubts about the whole thing. It comes with the territory known as love."

Springer was right, Quent decided late that night as he lay in bed. Love. He'd never felt this way, and he'd been a pure fool not to have made love to Cassie. What in the world had he been thinking? No, he countered thoughtfully. He'd been right. When they did finally come together, it will have been worth the wait. He pictured little Q.C., remembering again the thrill of holding his brand new little body in his hands. Maybe before too many years he would do the same for his own son. He'd see about the Snowden place tomorrow, he vowed.

Cassie told herself she should have more sense. Over and over she carried on a running argument with herself. And at times, late at night, the shadow of fear rose to haunt her. Good Lord, Quent was the man he was. There was no getting around it. She suspected that that was exactly what drew her to him.

But it wasn't practical.

Still, she continued to see him. She didn't break it off, and she began to harbor a tiny hope that perhaps it would be right, after all.

They met for lunch; Quent took her to dinner. They traveled to the city for a horse show; they observed nearly half the state from the helicopter. They spent one entire afternoon baby-sitting Q.C. Every day in the weeks that followed, Cassie spent at least a few hours with Quent, even if it was under the careful observation of Jesse as they sat and watched television.

And Cassie knew she was in love. She delighted in it; she savored it. The doubts and fears faded as adoration for Quent took their place. When she was with him, there was no room for shadows. There was only joy and her growing longing.

It was only when she'd see him in full uniform with the gun at his side that the negative emotions of doubt and fear managed to gain any hold at all. Then she was brought up quite squarely to the dangerous aspect of the job and of the man himself.

One day he caught her expression. She was standing, staring at the gun on his hip, unable to tear her eyes away.

He said her name twice before she heard. "What is it?" he asked, his eyebrows knotted together in concern.

"Nothing," she said, forcing a smile and moving into the comfort of his strong arms. "Nothing. Just daydreams." She rubbed her cheek against his soft shirt as if to rub the fear from her mind.

Quent took mostly night duty, and with his gift of a silver tongue, repeatedly succeeded in persuading Cassie to leave the store early in the afternoon. Many days she left with his hand tugging her from the store. At the same time she wondered why in the world she had said yes, why in the world she, Cassie Marlow, with perfect control of her life, wasn't able to resist him. Then she would look into his eyes and know. She wanted too much to be with him. A banked fire burned ever below the surface of their talk, hinting at a sexual attraction that she knew full well would not be forever denied.

On their third helicopter flight together, Quent decided to instruct Cassie in a few of the basics of piloting the steel whirlybird. The day was bitterly cold but crystal clear with a low wind, perfect for flying. Cassie delighted in the feeling of speeding through the air, at times just over the trees, at other times soaring up until the earth below resembled a patchwork design, yet close enough to always recognize where they were. She paid rapt attention to Quent's instructions, itching, as a child does, to do it herself. For once she was so engrossed in Quent's instructions that she forgot the sensual light in his eyes, and the wariness slipped momentarily from her heart.

"Lightly, Cass," he told her in his mellow easy voice, his guiding hand covering hers on the stick. "That's it." He flashed her an encouraging smile. Her heart twinged foolishly with pride.

Before she was even aware of it, he'd removed his hand, and for two fascinating minutes she had total control of the magnificent flying machine. It sent a surge of exhilaration through her veins. Glancing at Quent, she saw him looking warmly at her. The ever-present energy sparked between them.

Then the machine started to weave, tilting slightly. Cassie's heart jumped into her throat, but Quent only laughed, taking over the controls and immediately swooping down toward the earth in a smooth dip.

"You did fine, Cass," he said. "A few more times, and you'll be ready for a license."

Cassie gave a look that spoke clearly of her doubts. She turned her attention to the ground below as they sped over woods, pasture and a clay-dirt road. Following the dirt road, they passed above a large tractor-trailer truck. With a swift motion Quent veered away, then came back to pass over the truck, and yet again. He reached for the radio microphone, and Cassie sensed a tightness come over him as he spoke call numbers into the radio.

She thought she recognized the answering voice as Hadley Smith's, though it was hard to tell. Giving the location of the truck, Quent signed off.

"What is it?" she called to him over the engine noise.

Quent shrugged, calling back, "Maybe nothing. Just keeping an eye out. We've been watching for a truck like that. Could be poachers."

Cassie looked down the road, seeing the truck moving along at a slow pace and throwing up a red cloud of dust.

"In that?" she said, quite puzzled. She couldn't imagine how the huge truck and illegal hunting could be related. The poachers that she'd known of moved about the countryside at night in inconspicuous pickup trucks. Yet, at a second glance, the tractor-trailer truck did seem unusual, traveling off the blacktop highway. The trailer it hauled was enclosed, not an open cattle hauler.

"Could be a big operation," Quent told her as he swung the helicopter and headed in the direction of home. "Had it happen down south at the border to Texas last year, and we've found some of the same signs of it happening around here lately. Doing more than just putting food on the table—they're filling a refrigerator trailer, transporting it to the city and mixing it with ground beef to sell it."

Cassie shook her head at the audacious idea, but she'd seen enough outlandish and totally illegal enterprises to know it could just be possible. If it was in any way lucrative, someone was bound to try it.

A cool foreboding touched her spine. The enterprise was daring, and the people involved would not be the local countrymen, doing what they felt was their right at hunting. These people could be dangerous. Should they be caught, the penalty would be high; they would naturally do what they could to ensure that didn't happen.

Suddenly the haunting fear returned in full force, sweeping her stomach with nausea. When they landed, she pleaded a sick stomach from the flight and fairly bolted from the helicopter, wanting only to be alone, away from Quent's scrutiny. But with long strides, he caught up with her.

"Cassie?"

Catching her arm, Quent turned her to face him. The setting sun lit his features, and she saw the questioning in his golden eyes.

"It was just the dips," she said, pulling away. "I'll be fine in a bit."

She left him standing there, feeling her heart and stomach clench. She didn't want him to know, didn't want anyone to know. And she denied to herself the toll the excessive fear was taking. *Cassie Marlow was practical and levelheaded. She did not allow an emotion such as fear to dictate her life. She wouldn't! She simply wouldn't!*

When she'd made it to the bathroom, she was violently ill. And the tears that streamed from her eyes were not simply from physical reaction but came from her heart, as well.

The day came, of course. The weeks of simply being in his company, never thinking about taking another step, had to come to an end. Deep down Cassie had known it would, even though she had completely, and foolishly, refused to think about it. But it did come.

She recognized it the moment Quent stepped into the house and looked at her. She sensed the impatience written in the way he moved, just as in the weeks past she'd sensed his tight control. Much the same way that she could sense changes in her brothers, she could sense them in Quent, as well. It was like that, she supposed, when two people grew up together. She knew he could read her, too, though how well, she wasn't sure.

Quent took her to look at the old Snowden house.

"What do you think?" he asked as they stood looking around the kitchen. He shifted his weight from foot to foot. She smiled inwardly at his boyish countenance. "I could put in all new cabinets."

Cassie visualized the room as it could be, and saw herself in it. "There are four bedrooms," she said. Slipping close, she teased his mouth with a light kiss, secure in the knowledge that he wouldn't give in. He stood quite rigid and straight. For all the past weeks he'd only brushed kisses on her cheeks or forehead.

But then, emitting a low growl, Quent pulled her hard against his chest and kissed her. It frightened and thrilled her all at once. In a flash of honesty, Cassie admitted she'd been longing almost beyond endurance for his lips on hers. Their kiss deepened before Quent jerked away.

"You little shameless hussy," he drawled in his mellow voice, "you better be careful. You just might get what you're asking for." The gleam in his eyes attested to the truth.

Suddenly Cassie knew his thoughts, knew what he was about to say, and it terrified her.

"Cass, I'm sure now," he said. "I want to marry you. How about you?"

Even as she looked at him, her breath left her. Her gaze remained locked with his as her lungs burned. Then she gasped; air came in and went out, but she still felt she was strangling. There was just no air. She couldn't face Quent, and she couldn't understand what was happening to her.

"Cassie? Cassie, what is it?" Taking her shoulders, Quent forced her to face him. *"What is it?"* He gave her an impatient shake.

"I . . . can't . . . get my . . . breath," she managed, averting her eyes to the floor, embarrassed at the situation. It was nonsense, she told herself. Of course she could get her breath. Any moment. And still she gasped.

Quent took her arm and talked to her soothingly, as if she were a child, urging her to breathe in and out slowly. Leading her to where the warm sunlight spilled in through the windows, he sat her down on the floor. Gradually her normal breathing returned. She sat under his close scrutiny, wondering what had happened to her, suspecting, yet denying her emotions. They simply weren't rational. It wasn't like her at all.

"Better now?" Quent asked.

Cassie nodded. "Much."

He regarded her for a long moment, while outwardly Cassie remained quite still but inwardly squirmed beneath his gaze.

"Are you going to marry me, Cass?"

With all her heart Cassie wanted to say yes. But—she couldn't. And neither could she bear to face the fact that if she said no, she'd lose him forever.

She gave a reluctant shake of her head. "I—I need more time," she said softly, seeing the pain slip into his eyes. She touched his coat sleeve. "It's been good these past weeks. Hasn't it? Can't we just go on like this for a while longer?"

"Cassie," he said, eyeing her frankly, "you know it can't. And you know why. Neither one of us can hold out much longer. And I don't just mean sleeping together—I mean all that goes with it. I want it, and I believe you do, too."

"But..." She let the word trail off and took a deep breath. "I know what you're saying. But if you force me to choose now, I'll have to choose no. Please don't force me, Quent."

He held her gaze. He didn't blow up, didn't even look disappointed. In fact, he looked quite as though he was putting a puzzle together, triumphant in finding all the pieces.

"You're scared," he stated.

"I'm what?"

"You're scared," he repeated flatly. "I've seen it before, and I should have figured it out earlier, only fear is the one thing I've never associated with you. But then your father—"

"What has that got to do with us?"

"You're scared, aren't you?"

Cassie averted her gaze. "Maybe I am," she admitted. "A little bit. Marriage is a pretty frightening step. Anyone with a lick of sense has reservations about such a choice." She looked at him, and her voice softened. She didn't want to hurt him. Oh, Lord, she didn't want to hurt him. "This is a big choice, Quent, and I don't want to be pushed."

"Okay," he said pointedly, "So why would you choose no at this time?" He sounded like an inquisitor who was determined to get to the point.

Cassie rubbed her hands down her jeans, searching for the words. She needed to explain, needed to be truthful, yet it went so much against her grain to expose herself so completely.

"I told you this once before. I watched my father. I've watched Springer. I've known you since I was a child," she said. "I'm not sure I want to tie my life to yours because I know so well what all that will mean."

Quent's expression became unreadable. Cassie cringed inwardly when he rose and moved to the window, his back to her. He raked a hand through his hair.

"But you love me," he said.

"There's more to a marriage than love. Sometimes the facts of life can gnaw away until there's no more love left."

He turned to face her. "But you love me." Anger showed in his eyes and in his voice.

"I told you, there are practical things to be considered here. I don't want—"

Reaching out, he jerked her up to him and pressed his lips to hers, forcing her lips to part, kissing her angrily. Cassie thumped her small hands against his chest, pushing him away. Damn him! Brute force—it wasn't fair.

"You're scared!" he accused. "You're going to throw it all away because you're scared." Still he held her in his steely grasp, his eyes glaring just above her own.

"I am not! I'm making a choice!" she shouted at his accusation. It was her choice. Nothing and no one could force her to do anything she didn't want. *It was her choice.*

"No, you're not making a choice," Quent said, his voice very low. "You're letting an irrational fear make the choice for you."

"I am not!"

The air vibrated from the friction. Again Cassie's breath came short. She couldn't tear her gaze from Quent's. His eyes glittered with heat, and slowly, as if conducted by an invisible cord, the heat was transferred to her. She became aware of his body pressed against her own. With a measured movement he lowered his mouth toward her until she could no longer see it. Closing her eyes, she met his kiss.

The deliberate gentleness in his touch sent fire leaping in her veins. She clung to him, impatient with the heavy barriers of their coats. Quent fumbled with hers, his hands slipping inside, caressing her waist, then moving down to her hips.

"I love you, Cass," he whispered heatedly. His lips played upon her neck, his hands upon the swell of her breasts. "Marry me...marry me."

Cassie's heart beat wildly. She wanted to, she so very much wanted to. Oh, she couldn't think. All she could do was feel. She longed to lie with Quent, to know what it would be to make love to him. Forever.

"Quent..." She shook her head.

Roughly he placed his hands on her cheeks. She looked up into his golden-brown eyes.

"You want me?" he asked, giving a hint of a wicked smile.

Cassie nodded imperceptibly, allowing her eyes to speak for her.

"Then you're going to have to marry me, woman."

A hysterical chuckle escaped her throat. It was silly, preposterous. A man didn't say that to a woman. And yes, she wanted him.

"You can't say that," her words came breathlessly. "That's my line."

"I'm serious. If that's the only way I can get you, I'll do it," he threatened. "And you won't be able to keep away from me—you'll always be thinking about it, no matter what choice you think you've made."

"Don't push me, Quent." Anger nipped at her heart and trembled in her voice.

"Forget about the fear. Think about the love," he coaxed. He nibbled seductively at her lips. "And say you'll marry me."

"I'm not scared," she denied with an insistent whisper, her heart hammering. "And I won't be pushed." She had to break away, and yet he held her mesmerized by the vibrations tugging her to him. She did think about the love—saw it in his eyes—and yet she saw the threatening hint of the wild, untamed inner man.

No, she thought, *I can't say yes. I can't! I can't wait for him at night, wondering, worrying.* And she couldn't bear for him to see the fear.

She struggled out of his arms, aware of his tormented expression, but desperate to be away. She wouldn't be pushed. Not by Quent. Not by anyone.

"Cassie!" His footsteps echoed in the empty house as he ran after her. "Cassie!"

Chapter Ten

Her vision blurred by tears, Cassie ran across the meadow and into the woods along a faint trail instinctively remembered from childhood. On and on she ran, wild rose bushes and brittle oak limbs tearing at her clothes and hair. Finally, her lungs burning, she stopped and slumped against a tree, pressing her cheek to the rough surface of its bark. It was cool to her burning skin.

It was then she realized that Quent could have easily followed and caught her, but he'd let her go. She was grateful in that moment.

And yet pain touched her heart. It grew until it seemed to choke the very life from her.

It was over.

A whisper of doubt crossed her pain-dazed mind. Neither one of them had actually said they didn't want to see the other. He hadn't said that.

A hysterical chuckle tangled in her throat. Of course it was over. She'd just rejected the man's offer of marriage, actually ran away from him. Life for all these years with her brothers had taught her very well what his reaction would be. With a blow like that to his manly pride, Quent wasn't likely to come around offering to pick up the relationship as if nothing had ever happened.

And she didn't want that, she thought, giving a vehement shake of her head; she really didn't. It was over. She could face it. She would face it. It was best for them both.

Blinking and wiping at the tears that trailed down her cheeks, she looked around, as if seeing where she was for the first time. Resisting the powerful urge to curl into a ball on the cold cushion of oak leaves, she forced one foot in front of the other, again and again, and walked the rest of the way home. She opened the kitchen door with a numb hand, her thoughts miles away, seeking warmth in the memory of a day atop a sun-washed butte.

"Hi!" came an excited call, and Cassie looked up into the handsome smiling face of her brother Michael. Springer stood beside him, and Jesse slouched at the table. Slowly their smiles faded, an expression of shock and concern sweeping all their faces.

"Good Lord, what happened?" Springer bellowed.

Following his gaze, Cassie looked down to see the dirt smudges and bits of winter-dry leaves on her coat. She realized her hair was tangled, and with a tentative touch she pulled a dead leaf from her ponytail.

She couldn't tell them, couldn't explain. Not now, Cassie thought desperately. "I...I can't talk about it," she managed, and turned fleeing the men's inquiring faces.

Quent had waited as long as he dared. He wanted to give Cassie time alone, time to cool down, but now the sun was setting, and he had to make sure she'd made it home safe. His foot heavy on the accelerator, he pulled into the drive. It was a hell of a surprise to have Mike meet him on the porch.

"Hey, buddy." Mike grasped his hand eagerly as Springer stepped from the kitchen.

The greeting was warm, but Quent didn't miss the wary look in both men's eyes. "Hello, Mike." He was glad to see his friend, but other matters weighed on his mind. "Did Cassie come home?"

"Just a few minutes ago," Springer said, eyeing him uncertainly.

"Springer was just telling me about you and Cassie, Quent," Michael said. "I was pretty surprised. Then she comes running in here, crying, looking like she'd tangled with a tornado and lost. What happened?"

Remembering the pained expression on Cassie's face as she'd torn herself from his arms and run from the house, Quent winced inwardly and moved to push past the two big men.

"I want to see her," he said almost absently, intent on seeing Cassie. He wanted to hold her, to comfort her and remove that look of hurt.

But Mike blocked his way. "She's pretty upset. Said she didn't want to talk."

Trying to comprehend, Quent looked from Mike to Springer, who had moved to stand beside him. They resembled two bears guarding their cub and did not intend to let him pass.

"I want to talk to her," Quent said firmly.

"I can't let you do that now," Mike said, putting restraining hands on Quent's shoulders. "Now why don't you tell me what happened?"

Quent didn't know where to begin, and he didn't want to. This was a private matter between him and Cassie. Then, looking from Mike to Springer, he began to have a hint of what they could be thinking. Taking a deep breath, he struggled to keep his temper under control.

"What happened is between Cassie and myself," Quent said, looking Mike in the eye. "But I give you my word; I haven't hurt her."

"I didn't think you had," Mike allowed. "I just think you both better cool off. You can come back and talk to her a little later if you want to."

Quent looked at Mike for a minute, seeing eyes so like Cassie's—strong, vibrant, stubborn. "Okay," he said, giving a reluctant nod. Maybe it would be better. Mike and Springer had definitely made up their brotherly minds not to let him see Cassie without a fight, and his lying beaten to a pulp, with Mike and Springer maybe missing a few teeth, wasn't going to help matters.

"But I will talk to her," he added in a low voice.

As he turned to leave, Mike stepped up beside him and slapped a friendly hand on his shoulder. He looked at Quent for a long minute, then said, "Let's go for a few beer. You sure have the look of a man with woman trouble. Maybe between me and the beer, we can figure a few things out."

The room was dark. Cassie lay in her bed, wondering if she would ever be able to feel again. A curious numbness had settled over her. She found she could think of Quent and their times together in the past week and not feel anything. And that was perhaps more painful than sorrow.

A knock sounded at the door. "Cassie?" It was Jesse. "Cassie—come on. Open up. I've brought you something to eat."

Cassie sighed. She didn't want to get up, didn't want to face her brother or anyone else; she didn't want to move.

"Cassie," Jesse said more firmly. "I'm not leaving here until you open this door." He began an irritating rhythmic tapping on the door.

Giving in, she switched on the lamp and dragged her body from the bed. She opened the door, intent on telling Jesse she was fine and shutting it again. But the minute she opened the door, he pushed his way into the room.

"Brought you some warm milk and a piece of pie," he said matter-of-factly as he strode across the room and set the tray on the bedside table. He bent to prop up her pillows. "Come on...before the milk gets cold."

Somewhat awestruck by her younger brother's unusual attention, Cassie complied. When she sat on the bed, Jesse startled her by lifting her legs and tucking the covers around them. He'd never acted this way—taking care of her. None of her brothers had. Oh, they tried to boss her around about where she could and couldn't go, who she could and couldn't see, but none of them had ever done anything like this.

"I'm not ill, Jesse."

"Yeah, yeah. Just drink this stuff—don't know why you like it, but drink it, anyway." Forcing her to take the cup, Jesse sat on the side of the bed, not saying anything while she sipped the warm milk. He handed her the pie, and she nibbled on it.

"I just can't eat," she said, handing the plate back. Jesse didn't force her. Cassie was both touched and amused by the fatherly expression of concern on his young face.

"Cassie," he said, his expression suddenly betraying his boyishness, "I just want you to know I'm here if you need me. We all are."

His concern, unexpected and gentle, tore at her heart, and she blinked back tears. She touched his cheek. "Thank you," she managed in a hoarse whisper.

Then Jesse was hugging her. Clinging to his young strength, she felt the numbness that had insulated her heart cracking, allowing the pain to filter in, telling her that she was, after all, alive. And she cried.

When the tears had stopped, Jesse tucked her down into the bed and turned out the light. Immediately, and surprisingly, Cassie fell into a deep, drugging sleep.

Dreaming of a door, she tried so hard to open it, but it wouldn't open. She pounded and pulled, determined, even though she sensed that whatever lay behind the door was extremely dangerous. That didn't matter. All that mattered was getting the door open and facing whatever was behind it.

Then the door changed to a number of doors surrounding her, and she didn't know which one was the one she sought. They began to open and close, banging incessantly.

Gradually the banging penetrated Cassie's consciousness, and she realized it was actual noise. A sort of clumping and thumping mixed in. Someone was beating at her bedroom door.

Startled, she leaped from the bed, groping for the lamp in the darkness. The pounding had turned to a light tapping and then to silence by the time she'd crossed the room to the door.

When she opened it, a large male body fell from the darkened hallway against her.

"Quent!"

The realization startled her. Immediately she tried to support his limp body but was definitely outweighed. As gently as possible, she let him slip to the floor, cradling his head to keep it from hitting the bare oak surface.

In doing so, she found herself sitting on the floor, one of her legs pinned beneath her and Quent's head upon her lap. She stilled for a moment, looking at him, wondering what in the world had happened. She moved her hand to touch his cheek, then held it away in midair, her heart hammering.

His eyes were closed, his face muscles lax, with strands of hair falling across his forehead, giving him almost an innocent, boyish air. Cassie's heart tugged in longing. As though of their own accord, her fingers lightly brushed the stray hairs from his face.

His eyes flew open, and he looked at her. A crooked smile touched his lips.

"Couldn't find the light switch," he managed to slur out. He reeked of alcohol.

His eyes were very dark in the low light from the lamp. He blinked, fixing them upon her. "You're beautiful," he murmured. "You hair..." He waved his hand in the air. "Like it—hair—down."

He closed his eyes, and Cassie tried to move from beneath him. His eyes flew open again. "Aw, Cass. Don't be mad...I wanna talk. We can work it out."

Cassie smiled gently. "You've had too much to drink to try and talk."

He wrinkled his eyebrows, struggling to concentrate. "Don't be mad, Cass...don' be mad."

Cassie's heart warmed. "I'm not mad."

Then he gave that mellow grin that touched her soul. "Me and Mike..." He tried to brush her cheek, but missed. "Don't be mad, Cassie. I love you."

Then his eyes closed. Cassie sat there, his head heavy upon her lap, and listened as his breathing settled to the steady rhythm of sleep.

How gentle and innocent he looked. Not at all the big man, tough and strong. This was a side of him Cassie had forgotten even existed. How could she not have remembered? Just because he'd grown into an adult didn't mean this boyish, vulnerable part of him had ceased to exist. That didn't happen as people grew—generally, they just learned to deny and hide that part of them, but it didn't go away. It was there, still needing fulfillment.

Cassie stroke his forehead, knowing Quent wasn't about to awaken now. He'd be out for the night, she thought wryly, or what was left of it.

She looked at him, and amazement gradually slipped over her. He'd come to her. He'd actually come to seek her out after what had happened the past afternoon. She'd not expected it, not ever.

Could he really care about her so much? The thought kindled and flickered more strongly within. Maybe he'd been right, and she wouldn't be able to forget. And perhaps, no matter how wrong it was for them, they wouldn't be able to escape each other.

It was totally impractical, would end up hurting both of them, she countered the rising hope.

Ah, but she loved him, came a whisper into her despair, and he loved her. Perhaps they were a bit like oil and water—they didn't mix well together. But they weren't doing all that well apart, either.

Her emotions were a tangle of fear and yearning. They were both so headstrong, and she didn't like to be told what to do. But she loved being with him and longed beyond anything she could imagine to make love to him.

Oh, but the fear. It choked her throat. How would she survive the hours when she knew he was out there, doing who knows what? How would she survive if one day he didn't come home?

Well, she decided at last, sitting there wasn't helping her straighten out the jumble of confusing questions. With slow, stiff movements, she managed to extricate herself from beneath Quent's head. She got a pillow, limping to the bed and back on a numbed leg of pins and needles, and placed it beneath his head, then covered him with a blanket.

Quickly, as if to leave a piece of herself with him, she touched her lips to his.

Dressing hurriedly, she stuffed several changes of clothes into a bag. She stepped carefully over Quent, out the bedroom doorway, and quietly padded down the stairs. She didn't know where Springer was, Jesse still slept dead to the world, and she saw Mike sprawled on the living room couch.

In the kitchen she dialed the Reids' telephone number. A groggy Anita answered. Quickly Cassie told her plans but swore Anita to secrecy.

"You can call my brothers tomorrow and tell them I'm fine," she said. "Tell them I'll be home in a few days. But, Anita, don't give in and tell them where I am, no matter how much they badger you."

"What about Quent?"

"Don't you dare tell him, either."

"He's in love with you, Cassie."

"I just have to think about it, Anita," she said with a sigh.

"Well, if it were me, I wouldn't let a man like him slip through my fingers. And you're not getting any younger, Cassie."

"Thanks. That's just the sort of thing I need to hear right now."

"I was just pointing a few things out," Anita said flatly.

Cassie smiled wryly into the receiver. "Go back to bed, Anita."

Cork cast her an inquiring look, but Cassie shook her head. "Not this time, Cork."

Outside, she saw Springer's truck was gone, and a brief worry played across her mind. She shook it away. She simply had enough without that nonsense plaguing her.

She had to get away. Grover would look after the store, Lettie would manage with the house, and her brothers could certainly find their own socks for a change.

And Quent? What about Quent? How would her being gone affect him? Well, he didn't need her, not the way her brothers did. So, how did he need her? Maybe he didn't. The thought hurt.

Oh, Lord, she was so confused. The thought came out as a rather desperate prayer. She wasn't sure at this moment what she was feeling or even who she was. Turning on the pickup's lights, she pulled from the drive. She had to get away for a while to try to sort this all out.

Quent heard footsteps. He felt footsteps. They vibrated in his head. Then he heard someone calling his name. He tried to open his eyes, to figure out where he was, but he couldn't quite make it. Finally he managed to open one eye and saw Jesse Marlow's face blurred above him. He wondered why Jesse would be blurred.

"Quent, wake up," Jesse said. "Where's Cassie?"

Quent wondered why Jesse was bending over him. He blinked, and the boy's image cleared. He tried to move his head and discover where he was, but the movement sent a pounding through his head. He tried to think and remember, and that, too, caused unbearable vibrations.

"Quent, where's Cassie?" Jesse said again.

"Don't talk so loud, boy," Quent managed.

Gradually he realized he was lying on the floor, in—or half in—Cassie's bedroom. He stilled. Cassie's bedroom? On the floor? Thoughts tumbled over one another, and his memory stirred. He remembered talking and drinking with Mike and coming here intending to see Cassie. Slowly he tried to sit up. Jesse helped by pushing at his shoulders. There was a blanket over him, and his head had been lying on a pillow.

"Cassie?" Quent looked around the room. As if in a dream, he remembered. She'd had on a pink nightgown; her hair had fallen in a cascade across her shoulders, the vision of what Quent would term an angel. Had it been a dream? His eyes searched the room for proof of his fantasy. A pink nightgown hung across the foot of the bed. "She's not here?" He cast a questioning glance at Jesse.

Jesse shook his head. "I can't find her."

Quent allowed his shoulders to sag as any bit of lingering strength evaporated. He wanted to see her and talk to her, but she probably didn't want to see him at all now. He knew how she felt about drinking. She was probably madder than a hornet.

Cassie had driven to Quartz Mountain State Park, to stay in a cabin nestled away in the rocky hills. It was quiet there at this time of year. Why, it was under two weeks until Christmas, she realized, wondering how she could have forgotten. This weekend at home her brothers would have gone to cut the tree.

The sun was warm and bright, and Cassie spent hours walking over the rocky hills, thinking, absorbing the tranquillity of the land.

She loved Quent, of that she was sure. But would the love be strong enough to last through their inevitable disagreements? They were sure to have many.

Perhaps no one could ever tell that. You just had to take a chance. Did she want to? What was the alternative? She didn't want to face giving him up.

But what would happen to her when he went out on duty? Could she control the insatiable gnawing fear? Oh, Lord, the fear. She faced the fact that was what worried her the most. She'd tried for years to conquer it but had never fully succeeded. Would it overwhelm her and swallow her, tearing at Quent in the process?

She could hide it from him, she thought, grasping at the hope. Maybe she could. One thing was sure: her longing for him had begun to override the fear.

On the morning of the fifth day, she awoke and made ready to go home. She brushed her hair until it shone and left it loose. She would look for Quent before she'd go home.

He was working on the helicopter down at the police station, Marjean told her. He was dressed in grimy overalls, she saw when she drove up, and engine parts and tools were spread on the ground around him. He hadn't heard her approach.

"Quent?" she said shyly, stopping several feet from him.

His back stiffened, and then he turned. Joy hit Cassie as she saw the look of welcoming pleasure in his eyes.

"Hi, Cass," he drawled, his mellow smile breaking across his face.

"Hi."

They stared at each other. Cassie wasn't sure how to begin. But then Quent opened his arms, and she ran eagerly into his embrace.

He crushed her to him so hard he nearly took her breath. She rubbed her cheek against his chest. He smelled of grease and fresh winter wind. She heard his heartbeat.

"You're going to get greasy," he murmured as he brushed his cheek against her hair.

"Okay," she said, uncaring as she reveled in the feel of him.

Long seconds later he eased her away from him. Reaching for a rag, he wiped his hands. "So, where have you been?" The comment was light, but his gaze was penetrating.

"Over to Quartz Mountain. I needed to think."

Quent nodded. "And?"

Cassie took a breath. "I love you, Quent." She stopped, waiting for his reaction. Maybe he didn't want her now; maybe everything before had been a mirage.

"I love you too, Cass." His gaze narrowed, and a warm feeling passed between them. "Are you going to marry me?" he asked huskily.

Cassie glanced away. She'd thought she was prepared to face that question now, but she wasn't. The doubts of herself, of Quent, of them together, ran too deep. What could she say? She was still in the same position, caught between a rock and a hard place, that she'd been before she ever went away.

"Quent," she said, raising her gaze to his, "we don't have to get married." She stepped close and touched the placket of his overalls. "We're both adults."

He frowned. "Are you saying we can simply sleep together?" He sounded as if he'd never given it a thought.

"Why not? We can live together, Quent."

He looked somewhat stunned, as if she'd suggested they rob the Doyle City bank.

"Good grief, Cassie!" he said in a low voice and stepped back.

Cassie was astounded at his reaction. "What's wrong?"

"You, that's what's wrong. You tell me you've waited twenty-seven years to sleep with a man, and now you've suddenly decided to throw aside those principles."

"No—I'm living by those principles," Cassie said, irritated. "I've never been in love before. Now I am. And quite frankly, I don't find this in the least romantic, as I had always dreamed. I mean, listen to us. It's more like we're planning to attend a turkey shoot. And since when did you find such a suggestion repulsive and above you?"

Quent sighed. He touched her cheek. "I don't, Cassie. It just surprises me, that's all."

"Ah-ha!" she exclaimed before he could say anything else. "You still think of me somewhat as a little sister, don't you?"

"Well, maybe," Quent allowed, his voice rising. "I'm protective of you, okay? What's wrong with that? Is there something wrong with wanting to marry the woman you love?"

They glared hotly at each other. She could have told him or anyone else that they'd be like this. Then a chuckle twinged deep within Cassie. It was terribly funny. How often did a woman have trouble getting a man to go to bed with her?

"What's wrong? Don't I turn you on?" she asked with a chuckle.

Quent's lips twitched. She saw him fighting back a grin, but then it escaped. With a greasy hand he reached out and pulled her to him. "You know you do. When you look like that, you could turn a stone to water." His eyes twinkled. "Just where do you suppose we meet for this romantic rendezvous? Your house or my parents'?"

Cassie got his point and had to laugh out loud. They had no place to call their own, and it was thirty miles in any direction to a motel of any sort, and that idea had a drab appeal.

In a gesture of hopelessness, she threw up her hands, then let them drop. She walked several steps away from him, thinking, still chuckling wryly at the situation. Those four days she'd spent away hadn't helped one bit. She was still in the same position she'd been before she left. Afraid to say yes, unable to say no.

She glanced at Quent; he looked at her. They both looked away. Quent bent to pick up his tools. They clanged as he tossed them into his toolbox.

"What's wrong with it?" she asked, indicating the helicopter.

"Carburetor."

"Is it fixed now?"

Quent shrugged. "Think so." He rose, again wiping his hands on a rag, and gave a dry grin. "Guess I'll find out when I go up."

Irritation tugged at Cassie. "What kind of thing is that—finding out when you go up?" She didn't like the idea one bit. He should know beyond a shadow of a doubt. He could get hurt, could get killed, she thought anxiously, her gaze scanning his face, almost as if to imprint every minute detail in her mind.

Quent's eyes narrowed. "It's okay, Cassie," he said gently. "It's fixed. I just won't know if I need to work on it further until I test it. I'll still be able to get up and down."

She nodded, dropping her gaze, feeling terribly foolish. Her reaction had been all out of proportion.

His hair shone in the sunlight, and she longed to touch it. He looked at her, his eyes seeking answers. She saw him pondering, and she tried to think of a way out of her own confusion.

A gentle patience stole over Quent's expression. "How about if we just go back to where we were?"

"Where we were?" Cassie echoed, regarding him uncertainly.

"Yes." Stepping close, he gazed down at her. "Yes. I'm sorry I've been pushing you." He gave a half smile. "I ought to know better than try to push you into doing anything." He turned serious. "And this isn't something you should be pushed into. You'll know when you're ready."

She searched his face, not sure what to say.

"We need to talk about this, Cassie."

"Yes," she said, her gaze still on his face. Her heart trembled with relief, with joy, with questions. But she hadn't lost him. Not yet.

"I can't see you tonight." Quent gave a regretful frown. "I've got duty. But I'll see you tomorrow evening," he promised.

Disappointment tugged at her, but she smiled softly and nodded. "I have to go now—let them know I'm home."

Quickly, before she realized his intentions, Quent brushed his lips across hers. Heat flashed through her at the contact. She stared at him as he pulled away. A knowing look lit his eyes.

"I'll call," was his husky promise.

When she was halfway to her pickup, Quent called to her, and she turned.

"I bought the Snowden place," he said. There was something in his voice. A taunt? A promise? A hint? She couldn't be sure.

But she couldn't ask him because he waved to her, then rounded the helicopter and slipped into the pilot's seat.

Chapter Eleven

Quent watched Cassie. She hesitated, then returned to her pickup. But she was watching as he lifted the chopper. He skimmed the treetops, turning the machine away from town.

He hadn't intended to explain about buying the Snowden place, had deliberately waited until she'd walked away before he told her, hoping to tease her with something to think about.

They could fix it up together, he thought, and if she wouldn't marry him, at least she'd said she was willing to live with him. Mike, Springer and even Jesse may come after his hide, but if that was the only way it could be for a while, that was it. He loved her; he wanted her. And they would be married, he affirmed. He was just going to have to be patient.

It had been unfair, even childish, to try to push her into marrying him, and it had been stupid, as well. A person couldn't push Cassie into doing something; she'd back up all the way like a stubborn mule. But, like a mule—and he smiled at the comparison—he could perhaps lead her. He

might as well learn early how to deal with her, if he planned
to live the rest of his life with her.

He'd begin by getting her to talk to him. They needed to
talk. If he could understand her reasons for hesitating about
marrying him, then he could help her understand them.
After his long and somewhat fuzzy talk with Mike, Quent
had more insight into what Cassie had seen of her parents,
especially her mother, while growing up. Now he needed to
get Cassie to see.

That Quent had bought the Snowden place surprised her.
That it was barely a mile down the road from her own home
made her sort of tingle. But what really kept returning to
tantalize her was the way he'd told her about it. He'd done
it on purpose, she thought wryly. He'd told her like that and
then had flown off, knowing she'd wonder just what he
meant by it.

She did wonder. Could it be that he intended for that to
be a place for them? Perhaps he wasn't so adverse to them
living together, after all. She thought of her brothers. They
would not take this lightly. Not at all.

When Mike, Springer and Jesse had all come home that
afternoon, and after Cassie had paid sufficient penance for
leaving as she had, she urged all three of the men out door
to find and bring back a Christmas tree before dark. Mike
planned to return to Denver the following day, and she
wanted them to decorate the tree together as a family before he left.

It was a gay time, a time of doing all the traditional
things: testing the lights and finding one bad bulb on every
string; unwrapping keepsake ornaments and retelling their
stories; drinking hot apple cider; and Springer, being the
tallest, setting the treetop angel and falling into the tree. He
did that every year.

The family joy and love flowed over Cassie like a sooth-
ing blanket. If only Quent were there, it would have been
perfect. Repeatedly her thoughts were drawn to him, and to
his carefully spoken comment about buying the Snowden

place. Several times she found herself gazing out the window in the direction of the Snowden house, though she couldn't see it. Her blood grew warm with longing as Quent's image slipped before her mind's eye.

She wanted to marry him, she really did. But she needed to get in touch with herself first and straighten out her feelings of fear. Until she did that, she wouldn't be good for him, wouldn't have anything to give him. It wasn't Quent she doubted; it was herself. And until she could trust herself... Trust herself to do what? Not come apart at the seams and make his life a living hell by her constant dread and fear? That was it. At last she'd admitted it straight out. Until she was sure of herself, she couldn't give him the full commitment that he wanted.

He called her twice. Once early in the evening, then later, before she went to sleep. He lingered on the line, as if he loathed to let her go. She felt the same. They didn't speak of anything important, just idiotic little comments to hear each other's voice.

The second time, Cassie managed to have the courage to ask Quent about the Snowden place. He'd closed the deal two days earlier, he told her. Again it wasn't what he said, but the way he said it. She knew he was deliberately teasing her, though she hoped to pay him back by refusing to ask anything more. How well he knew her, Cassie realized.

Where was he? she wondered as she tossed and turned, unable to sleep. Was he driving back into town? Had he stopped to investigate an empty car he didn't recognize? Her imagination skittered away with dark thoughts. She pictured the roads as they were at night deep in the country, dark, lonely, isolated. That was his world. At times, she knew, that world was a most wondrous place. It gave a man such as Quent the freedom he needed—no walls hemming him in, no strangling timetable, no boss breathing down his neck. It gave him a way to be close to nature, in tune with it.

And at times it could be extremely dangerous.

She fell into an uneven sleep, tossing with distorted dreams of the time when her father had died.

Quent telephoned early the next morning, speaking first to Mike to say goodbye and wish him a good trip. Cassie was relieved and irritated at herself for that relief. She hadn't needed to be one bit worried. Good grief, she scolded herself, rangers were not gunned down everyday. It was a rare occurrence—like eclipses of the sun. He'd been out on a simple patrol, simple and everyday.

After his goodbye, Mike handed the receiver to Springer. So she would be third, Cassie chuckled good-naturedly. Hearing Springer speak the name *Orin Donner*, her ears pricked up. Springer glanced at her, then turned his head and lowered his voice. Knowing she shouldn't be listening, and truly trying not to, she moved to finish gathering snacks for Mike to take on his trip.

Springer's low-toned mumbles floated across the room to her. She couldn't hear what he said, but a cool foreboding settled over her. Orin Donner was a rough sort, had been in trouble before, and Springer definitely didn't want her to know what he was talking about.

When next Springer looked at her, he held the receiver out, indicating it was her turn. He smiled wickedly. "Quent said if you just had to, he'd talk to you," her brother teased.

Pulling a face, Cassie took the receiver from him.

"Good morning, Cass." Quent's warm voice came across the line.

"Hello." Their words seemed to hang in the air. Was he picturing her, as she was him?

Springer didn't leave. He moved closer and began making faces at her. She pushed at him, but he only laughed as he reached out to tickle her.

"I'll be at the store around two," Quent told her suddenly, almost gruffly.

"I've been away five days," she protested. "I'll have mountains of work to catch up on. Will you stop it?" she burst out, trying to fend off Springer's hands.

"What's going on?" Quent asked.

"I didn't mean you...." She giggled as Springer tickled her. "Springer's tickling—me. Springer! Let me talk."

"You watch it with my sister, Romeo!" Springer teased, speaking loud enough for Quent to hear. Then he slipped from the room as Cassie hurled a hot pad after him.

"I owe him one," Quent vowed into the telephone. "And when I get my hands on you, I don't plan to be tickling."

Right there in the middle of her kitchen, Cassie blushed. She was glad no one was there to see.

"Be ready at two," Quent said again.

Cassie thought she caught a muffled chuckle in his voice. No doubt he imagined the effect his words had on her. Her womanly pride came to the fore, and she repeated, "I'll have too much work." She didn't want him to think she would just drop everything the moment he beckoned.

"I don't care," Quent growled. "I'll be there. I need to see you." His voice came across the line low and husky with desire.

Cassie weakened. She felt the same; there was no denying it.

"Me, too," she allowed in a soft voice. Again she remembered his comment about the Snowden place.

As she'd foreseen, there was a ton of work waiting for her at the old store. Invoices and receipts practically overflowed her desk where Grover had tossed them. He handled very little of the monetary transactions. There was bookkeeping to catch up on, bills and banking. And yet, Cassie found herself looking at the clock, willing the hands to turn to two o'clock.

What strange affliction, she wondered, invaded a perfectly sane and intelligent woman such as herself and made her act so totally foolish? She sighed, giving a reluctant knowing smile. It was called love, and it was wondrous, nerve-racking, exciting and terrifying in its intensity. It was changing her life, leading her in directions that she knew full well would be challenging and dangerous—to her heart.

When Quent came, something within, pride no doubt, prodded her to protest of the work still needing to be done.

"And Grover has been working alone long enough," she said, sounding perfectly logical.

Before she realized his intent, Quent's arm snaked out, and he grabbed her, astounding her by kissing her right there in front of Grover and a customer. A full, no-nonsense kiss as he pressed his hard length against her body. The contact took her breath away. When he broke away, she looked up into warm bobcat-sly eyes, twinkling with both humor and something else. Desire.

"Aw, go on, Cassie," Grover urged her, his face split into a wide grin.

Quent reached for her coat. Mrs. Crawford, the customer, had quite a look of shock, which suddenly turned to rich amusement, much to Cassie's sinking dismay. She and Quent had probably made the woman's day.

Nodding to the woman, Cassie said to Grover, "See that Mrs. Crawford gets that catalog on beekeeping I was telling her about. I can get you those bees in just a few days, Mrs. Crawford," she promised to the woman over her shoulder as Quent hurried her from the store.

The sun was bright in a cold sky. A band of blue to the north hinted that the weatherman's prediction of snow could very well be accurate.

"Where are we going?" Cassie asked as she slipped into Quent's pickup. It was his patrol truck, and the set of radios in the middle below the dash kept her from sitting close beside him.

Smiling and giving a slight shrug, he took her hand. "Someplace where we can be alone."

Cassie suspected that was the Snowden place, thinking to herself that they would have to begin calling it the Hatfield place.

A quietness enveloped them, not tense, but rather smooth and easy, a sharing that went beyond the need for words. Cassie's thoughts flitted from the beauty of the countryside to the Snowden place, to memories of her and Quent as children. What did Quent plan for them in the moments to come? What did she? Why didn't she just speak to him about these wonderings? But she couldn't.

He wasn't in uniform, but the crackling of the radio, left low for monitoring, and the long rifle in the rack above her head were stark reminders of his occupation and of the fear that tugged at her constantly.

They passed her own home and moments later pulled up the long overgrown drive to the small clapboard house Quent had just purchased.

Cassie knew that when Quent left his radio on, with the pickup's doors open, he was listening for a special message. Springer had often done the same. She started to speak to him about it, but he kissed her lightly, then led her to the meadow adjoining the yard and began describing his plans for the farm.

Christmas trees, he told her, needed irrigation that he'd have to set up. Then he spoke of methods of improving the soil to make it favorable to grow a type of tree that preferred cooler temperatures than what central Oklahoma offered. They checked out the two ramshackle barns, each of them deciding the barns were beyond repair.

Cassie saw in Quent both the boy she remembered and had known well, and the striking, confident man he'd become. She delighted in watching the reflection of the sun in his eyes and listening to his mellow voice. For these moments, she felt free from any doubts or fears, any commitments and decisions. They were just there, together, sharing precious moments suspended in time.

Picking a single long blade of fluffy grass, Quent tickled the skin below her ear. When he moved as if to kiss her, Cassie swiftly darted away, laughing, and the chase was on. With long legs pounding, she ran behind cedar trees to hide until he spotted her, then darted off again just as he was about to reach her.

Then unexpectedly he stepped out in front of her, and she ran right into his arms, throwing them both off balance. Laughing, they tumbled to the thick, winter-browned tufts of grass.

Struggling to catch her breath, Cassie opened her eyes to see Quent's only inches from her own. Their golden-brown depths held laughter, but in seconds Cassie watched that laughter ebb from his eyes and heat take its place. Heat that seemed to reach out and draw her to him. Instinctively she parted her lips for his kiss.

His mouth crushed hers in a demanding kiss. At first the fierceness jolted Cassie, taking her breath away. The next instant Quent gentled slightly, massaging her lips, questioning, seeking with his kiss, breathing sweet heat into her body.

Wondrous sensations pulsed through her veins, sweeping her along with their enticing warmth. She savored them, trying to grasp and hold them, wanting more. A deep longing flickered, then quickly throbbed throughout her whole being. Somehow her hands, drawn by the warmth, found their way inside Quent's coat. The muscles of his back were smooth and hard beneath his flannel shirt. Again and again she rubbed her hands over his back, delighting in the feel of him.

She moved against him, driven by natural instinct to satisfy the longing of her body and her heart. A mist of pleasure enveloped her. She no longer thought, only felt.

"Cassie..." he murmured.

His voice beckoned her back, calling her to think. No, she didn't want to leave the sweet warmth of the sensual world she'd discovered.

"Cassie," Quent said again, tracing light kisses upon her silky cheek. He pulled back to watch her face, seeing the struggle written there. The longing was deep within him, but this was no place, the hard cold ground in winter. What in the world could he have been thinking?

He traced her sleek jawline with his finger, and her eyes fluttered open. They were large and round, the crystal color of the sky, and held the heat of a summer day. She blinked, and he saw her trying to focus. Her eyes widened, realization dawning clearly in them.

Teasingly Quent stroked his thumb across the bare skin covering her ribs. She trembled at the touch, regarding him with a look of awe. He knew she'd not realized until that moment that his hand had found its way under the bulky coat and unbuttoned her blouse.

Smiling at her expression, he again stroked her skin and delighted in the heat that slipped into her blue eyes. But, he told himself reluctantly, he couldn't sit here all day playing games. Sitting up, he pulled her onto his lap. They looked at each other for a long minute, as if sharing their longing. The desire written so plainly in her eyes made him feel like one hell of a man, kindling a feeling of tenderness and protectiveness he'd never experienced before.

Slowly, deliberately, he rebuttoned her blouse. His hands shook slightly, and his knuckles brushed her skin. Cassie sat quietly, extremely feminine beneath his ministrations, unembarrassed by the action. The knowing went deep between them. Then he cradled her against him, and it was as if an invisible web encircled and held them together in a cocoon all their own. Cassie trembled against him.

"You're cold," he said, touching her chin and tilting her face toward him.

Cassie smiled beguilingly. "No—"

His loins tightened. "Ah, Cassie, you should be ashamed of your wanton ways." He allowed himself a low chuckle.

"I should?" She raised an eyebrow.

"No," he replied after a minute, his eyes studying her face. "No," he repeated. He moved to lift her. "Come on. This is not the best place to be making love. I don't care to have a coyote sniffing around and observing us."

His arm tight around her, they walked to the truck. It seemed colder; hazy clouds filtered the sunlight. Quent started the truck and turned on the heater. He thought uncertainly about how he felt, what he wanted to do. Cassie nestled into the crook of his arm, stretching her legs to the far side. Impatient with the crackling from the radio, Quent turned it down.

"I thought I'd begin painting the inside of the house next week," he told her. Her hair was like spun silk beneath his cheek. "Do you want to live here with me?"

"Yes." There was hesitation in her voice. Quent, himself, wasn't satisfied with the idea; he'd never lived with a woman, had never intended to. But if it had to be that way for now, it would do.

He started the engine, turned the pickup back down the drive and drove out onto the road. When he came to the Marlow farm, he pulled into the drive. He let Cassie look at him with wide eyes for a moment before he said anything.

"Well," he said, a reluctant grin slipping out, "there's no one here. Right?" Opening his door, he stepped from the truck. Cassie just sat there, watching him with her vivid blue eyes as he rounded the cab and opened her door. "Well?" He waited, seeing the longing and uncertainty flicker across her face.

Instinctively, knowing what he wanted, he pulled her to him, kissing her, flitting his tongue into the warm recesses of her mouth, promising more. Vaguely he heard the low crackling of the radio. She tasted sweet, oh, so sweet, and he remembered clearly the feel of her skin beneath his palm and the swell of her full breasts. Desire overwhelmed him, and it came to him firmly that he'd waited long enough.

But suddenly Cassie struggled against him. "Quent," she said breathlessly. "The radio."

"What?" he growled, seeking her mouth.

"The radio. I think that's Springer calling you."

He heard it then. It was Springer, his voice crackling faintly over the radio. *"Damn!"* Quent issued the oath in disgust and frustration. Glancing at Cassie, he took in her flushed face and the pulse beating in the hollow of her creamy throat.

He was sorely tempted to turn the radio off, his need overshadowing everything else. But he'd told Springer he'd be available. *Why in heaven's name had he done such a stupid thing— Because it was his job, and Springer was his friend.* His gaze lit upon Cassie's red, moist lips. They were parted slightly, waiting. He felt her whole body waiting for him. Slowly her arm reached for him, and he leaned toward her, Springer's call halfway forgotten.

But then the radio crackled again with his name, and they both jumped.

"Damn!" Quent swore again, reaching impatiently to the radio, turning the volume up and jerking the microphone from its hook. "Yeah, Springer. Come in."

As he listened for Springer, Quent slipped a hand into her coat and stroked her waist. Shivering slightly at the touch, Cassie looked up to see Quent smile knowingly at her.

"Come in, Springer," he said again into the microphone, though his gaze remained on her.

"Yeah, Quent," came Springer's voice, clear and loud now. "Did some checking, and we think you're right about Orin Donner. 'Course it didn't take much guessing. He's been at it before. Got the search warrant. How about coming out with me?"

At the words *search warrant*, an icy cold swept down Cassie's back. Search warrant. The words echoed in her brain in capital letters. To Cassie it meant desperate people, resistance, guns. Her father had gone that day, so many years ago yet only yesterday, it seemed, to serve a warrant and had been killed.

Averting her face from Quent's, she listened as he told Springer he was on his way and would meet him in town in ten minutes.

"I'm sorry, Cass," Quent said, dejection coloring his voice as he pressed his face into her hair and kissed her neck. He shuddered against her. "Lord, I'm sorry."

She turned her head, searching for his lips, kissing him fiercely. For a moment she considered asking him not to go. He didn't want to, she thought wildly. *She could get him to go into the house with her, make him forget all about the warrant as they made love.*

Then gently, he unwound her arms from his neck and regarded her closely. She moved her gaze over his features, holding each one in her heart—his golden-brown eyes, so warm, so sensuous in that moment, the sharp planes of his cheeks, his thick burnished mustache.

"Cassie, I'll be all right," he said slowly. "And we'll furnish the house—our house—before Christmas. That's a promise."

She nodded, smiling brightly. His gaze narrowed, but he only said, "I'll take you back to your truck at the store." A minute later he was backing the pickup swiftly from the drive.

"Has Orin Donner been poaching again?" Cassie asked after a moment, forcing her voice to remain lightly curious.

Quent nodded. "I spotted his pickup last night—him driving, I think. Cut in front of me as he flew out of a cutoff from Turner Road. When I went tracking down the cutoff into the woods, I found the hind-quarters of a butchered doe." He gave a snort of disgust. "Couldn't be bothered with taking the whole thing, I guess."

"This won't be the first time he's been caught," she said. If convicted, Orin Donner would lose any and all his guns, any and all pickup trucks, and they wouldn't be returned. And jail. It was enough reason for a man to resist arrest, especially if it looked as though the charge could be proven.

"I know." Quent sighed. She caught his glance. "It's okay, honey." Her heart trembled. It was the first time he'd used such an endearment. He winked. "You can count on me for dinner. And maybe we can induce Springer and Jesse to go to the movies or something."

"I don't think they will leave us alone at the house," Cassie quipped, seeking to match his easy banter, to hide the fear seeping into her bones. Images flashed before her mind: a menacing, distorted rifle, a puddle of blood, Quent's smiling face, the rifle again.

"Then we'll drive into the city tomorrow night," Quent said as he pulled to a stop in the parking area of the feed store. Taking her chin in his hand, he turned her head and studied her eyes. "I love you. Springer and I are going to be fine. I'll call you just as soon as we get back in town."

She forced a smile, then brushed a kiss across his lips and hopped from the truck. Walking up the steps to the store, she heard the crunch of tires on gravel as he drove away.

The store was empty. Cassie found Jesse and Grover playing checkers in the back. Grover smiled knowingly and Jesse looked curious. No doubt Grover had told her younger brother about her and Quent's encounter earlier in the afternoon.

"Didn't stay long," Grover commented.

Cassie ignored the comment. "Thought you were supposed to work after school," she told Jesse.

"We did it all," he said. "Thought you were supposed to work this afternoon."

She saw his teasing grin and smiled back automatically, but her mind was on Quent and Springer, even as she swept a hand across Jesse's hair. Wandering back to the front of the store, she sat at her desk. She tried totaling sales for the day, finding business had been brisk the few hours between the time she'd left and returned.

She wondered if they'd left town immediately. How long would it take them to reach the Donner farm? And with a start Cassie found she'd been staring into nothingness, her hand clutching the invoices so hard that she'd wrinkled them.

Suddenly she rose and grabbed her purse and coat. She had to see for herself. *She had to make sure Springer and Quent were all right.* The fact that what she intended was not only reckless and irrational, but would also infuriate the two men, didn't matter. The fear was clawing at her heart and mind, tearing her to pieces. *She wouldn't, simply couldn't, sit there and do nothing.*

With long swift strides she left the store, banging the door behind her. It was only fifteen minutes at the most, she calculated, to Orin Donner's. She shouldn't be too far behind Quent and Springer. Her truck tires flung gravel as she sped up onto the blacktop road leading through town. Icy slivers of moisture began to fall upon the windshield.

Chapter Twelve

Cassie switched on the wipers once to clear the windshield, then switched them off as her mind turned anxiously to what she knew of Orin Donner. Her impressions of him were not in the least reassuring. He had a running bill at the feed store, and she had never pressed for full payment. She'd wanted to often enough, but felt it would be unfair to press him when she let the others ride.

He was heavyset, with a protruding belly, and slatternly. He always looked as though he'd been in the field digging with his bare hands, yet Cassie doubted by the look of his place that the man did any actual work. He spoke little and then coarsely, and the glances he gave Cassie often made her ill at ease, as if he were peeking beneath her clothes.

She didn't think he was an evil man, but she suspected by the harsh way he treated his wife that he could be cruel. And he was proud and defiant, unyielding to the laws that he felt obstructed his personal liberty. Such as shooting deer, as many and as often as he chose and on whomever's land he wished. Springer also had mentioned that he believed Orin

Donner had a little business on the side stealing and reselling tractors.

Anxiety gripped Cassie as she swung the shiny pickup off the blacktop and down a sandy clay road. Again she had to sweep the windshield free of a spattering of sleet. She tossed her hair back, pressing the accelerator hard. The back end of the pickup skidded across the thickening sand and churned dust behind.

Cassie strained to see, looking for Springer's and Quent's trucks. As she approached the Donner farm, she saw them parked to the side of the road, Springer's first, then Quent's, ahead by several yards. The Donner yard sloped upward to a ramshackle house at the top of a rise.

The next instant Cassie was shocked to hear a gunshot ring out and to see a tall form jump behind Quent's truck. It was Springer.

Quent. Oh, Lord, please. Where was Quent? Had the shot—

Without thinking, she pulled her truck behind Springer's, jerking to a stop, then opened her door and got out to peer past the trucks. There was another shot, the sound jolting Cassie's body and ripping through her heart. For an instant shock paralyzed her. Frantically her gaze searched the yard behind the trucks for Quent. She moved forward, every sense straining to locate him while shadowy images of a man's body lying upon the ground swept through her mind.

"Okay, Donner." Springer's voice drew her attention. He had a rifle trained above the bed of Quent's truck toward the house. "Give it up. You're not going anywhere."

In answer, a shot sounded from the house and pinged against Quent's truck.

Fear and urgency choked in Cassie's throat. She couldn't see Quent. Where was he? Reaching the front of Springer's truck, she ran forward, stepping into the yard itself, her eyes searching the bushes, discarded barrels, dilapidated tractor parts, and an old trailer.

"Cassie!" Springer yelled behind her. At the same time from the house, Donner shot his gun toward a galvanized watering tub for cattle at the far end of the yard. *Quent! He was there behind it!* He turned to stare at her, though she couldn't fully see his face in the distance that separated them.

Foolishly she stared at the water spout squirting from the tub in the wake of Donner's shot, and angry outrage rose like a spewing fountain within her. Her heart pounded and all her thoughts focused on one thing—getting to Quent, touching him.

"Cassie, get the hell out of here," Quent yelled.

"Stop it!" she screamed, hot fury forcing her boldly into the yard. Oh, how she hated this violence! Stupid, needless violence! And yet she felt she would very much like to claw at Orin Donner at this moment, and perhaps the whole world, as well. She just wanted it to stop, for Quent and Springer to be safe. "Orin Donner, you stop it right now!"

There seemed to be a lot of yelling all around her, but heedless of all else, Cassie continued striding in the direction of the water trough.

The next instant the front door of the house opened a crack. A rifle came flying out past the porch and landed in the yard. "I ain't shootin' at no woman," Orin Donner called. "I'm coming out. I'm coming out."

He was safe. Quent was safe. Her spirit soared with relief, and she ran to him to touch his arm and look into his face. He was safe, was all she could think at first. And then his hot anger registered in her mind.

His eyes glittering, his jaw taut, he ground out, "What in the hell are you doing here?"

It was like a slap across her face, yet even as the pain of rebuke sliced into her heart, Cassie knew she'd been wrong.

How could she have done such a thing? she thought in horror. She just hadn't been able to control it. *The fear—it had taken over, forcing her. She just couldn't stand sitting helplessly in the clutches of that fear. Not this time.*

Oh, Lord, what could she say to him? Pure disgust poured from his eyes, shriveling her spirit.

Gripping her arm above the elbow with one hand and carrying his rifle with the other, he marched her along beside him as he walked rapidly to the trucks at the road. She went along numbly, having to run to keep up with his long, swift strides, feeling as if her spirit were leaking away through a giant hole in her heart.

Springer was handcuffing Orin Donner. He cast a worried glance at Cassie and then at Quent. "I'll take him in," he said.

"I never intended to shoot no woman," Orin Donner mumbled. "I didn't, either. You can't say I did."

Barely breaking his stride, Quent tossed Springer his rifle. "Keep this," he growled, "I've got some business with her." Cassie tried to pull her arm from his grasp, but he tightened his grip.

Quent pulled her along to her truck, then roughly spun her to face him. "What did you mean by coming out here?" he raged.

He towered over her, his face a mask of fury. But at least he's alive, she thought wildly. Oh, Lord, what had she done? How could she explain?

"I was frightened—" she tried to say.

Quent shook his head and looked away, as if he couldn't bear the sight of her. The painful rent in her heart widened. It wasn't possible for them. How could she ever had thought it could be? She was warped by this fear she couldn't control, and it would humiliate him and tear him apart—just like her mother's had her father.

"I'm sorry," she murmured, dropping her gaze. Her heart cried out her sorrow.

"Why, Cassie?" he asked plaintively.

"I was afraid. You could have been hurt."

"I could get hurt crossing the street in broad daylight."

"But he was shooting at you!"

"Yes. But there were several hundred gallons of water between me and him. Maybe if he'd truly intended to shoot

me, he could have. I don't know. But it goes along with the
territory. It's part of the job, and it probably won't be the
last time I'm shot at. But I know what I'm doing, Cassie.
Believe it or not, I'm not a fool. I do know what I'm
doing!"

"I know that!" Cassie's voice rose to match his. "I didn't
say you didn't. And stop yelling at me!" Sobs broke her
voice. "I hate this." She gestured into the air, feeling the
truth of herself that she'd held in secret for so long bubbling up and out. "I'm terrified. All the time. Just when I
think it's gone, the horrible fear and dread return to nag at
me. I'm terrified that something will happen to you." She
swept her arm toward her brother. "To Springer. And yes,
sometimes I'm terrified for Mike and Jesse. I hate it! I hate
it!" He grabbed her arms as she pounded her fists against
his chest while great sobs racked her body. "I hate it. I'm so
afraid. I'm—I'm sorry."

His arms went around her, supporting her as she slumped
to his chest. The pain of remorse and regret overwhelmed
her. She loved him, but she couldn't ruin his life by marrying him. She'd be a burden. He'd know her fear. It could
even get him killed.

Then he shook her, forcing her to look up at him. His eyes
were dark pinpoints in the evening's growing dimness.
"Cassie," he said, forcing her to look at him. "It's okay. I
know. I understand your fear. We can face it together—but
not like this."

She tore away from him, shaking her head. "He could
have shot you. Could have killed you! And you don't understand anything." She practically spit the words at him.
"Are you the one that remains patiently behind, waiting?
Do you ever have to worry about the one you love out doing
insane things like this? All my life I've lived with men who
weren't content unless they were out riding bulls, or buffa-
loes." Her thoughts came out as so much gibberish, but she
continued on. "Or tearing up the countryside in their trucks
and motorcycles, until they'd broken nearly every bone in
their body. Mike has, you know. One doctor told him he'd

be lucky to walk if he broke another. And Springer—letting people shoot at him. And Jesse. Who knows what he'll do. And Daddy..." Tears streamed down her cheeks. She blinked to clear them, seeing Quent's face through a blur. "Momma watched the window all the time." She couldn't explain the hurt and fear and remorse in her heart.

"Cassie. I know." Quent's voice dropped. He reached for her, but she stepped away, not wanting his touch, not daring to feel his touch in that moment. "I was terrified for you only minutes ago," he continued. "I was afraid Donner was going to shoot you. I understand. And it's okay to be scared. But not to let it control your life—our lives."

"Do you think I don't know that?" she threw at him. "I know it! I do! I've tried to control it, but it just grows and grows until I can't think straight anymore."

"But you've been trying to do it all alone, Cassie. You've held it in until it's gotten all out of proportion." He reached for her, and this time she allowed him to take her arm. "Share it with me, Cassie. Together we can get it under control."

She looked at him, wanting to listen, wanting him to have some answers. He looked back.

"I can't," she said at last. "This thing will only bring you pain. You'll worry about me so much you won't be able to do your job. And then you'll begin to hate me. I saw my mother shrivel away and die, and somehow she took a piece of my father with her. I won't do that to you. I won't do it to us."

Quent took her arms and shook her. She felt limp, like a rag doll, and a terribly deep and sad acceptance settled over her. She'd have to let Quent go; she never should have believed that it would work between them. She brushed the tears from her cheeks, and no more came.

Quent's expression hardened. "What do you want? Me to quit the rangers?"

For a moment, Cassie closed her eyes against the pain. "No," she said, barely above a whisper. She gave a soft, sad smile. "I'd never want to change you. Never. And it would never work, anyway.'' Her shoulders sagged, as if all her life had drained away. She turned to her truck.

Quent stepped after her, jerking her around to face him. "You can't do this. I won't let you. We will talk about it.''

"I don't want to," she said. "I've lived enough with my brothers not to live the rest of my life bouncing from one scare to another with you. I won't. And I won't let you do something you'll regret!''

Tugging her arm from his grasp, she opened the truck door, slipped inside and slammed it behind her. Every motion was automatic as her mind struggled to function through a mist. With blurred vision she saw Quent standing in the middle of the road where she'd left him, staring at her. There was pain on his face, despair and disbelief.

Oh, my darling, she thought, I didn't mean much of what I said. I didn't mean to sound so hateful. But she had meant what she said about it being impossible for them. It was.

She eased the truck past him; he didn't move. Moments later she became aware of sleet falling heavy and hard against the windshield, and that her face and hair were coldly damp. She was so cold.

Quent stood there watching her drive away, then he turned his eyes heavenward, letting the cold sleet pelt his hot, furious face. Then he kicked angrily at the sandy road.

How in the world had they gotten from their loving afternoon, when they couldn't keep their hands off each other, to this? What in the hell had possessed the woman? He still couldn't quite believe what Cassie had done. He pictured the entire scene: Cassie walking bold as day into Donner's yard, hardly even looking at the house, as though the man wasn't there with a gun. No, only looking at him, intent on him. He couldn't help it. A chuckle cracked through the hard wall of anger.

Oh, Lord, Cassie was one of a kind, he thought somewhere between annoyance and grudging admiration. She'd felt something so strongly that it got her to the point of doing something about it.

Slowly Quent walked back to his pickup, his anger fading into grim determination. If Cassie thought she was having the final say about this relationship, she was in for a big surprise.

And he had an edge. It wasn't as if they'd only known each other for a courtship of a few months—he'd known Cassie since she'd had to stick her foot out for him or Mike to tie her shoe. Granted, he hadn't been around her the past few years, but what he knew of her counted for a lot.

He knew she'd cool down and think over what had happened, just as he was doing. He searched his mind, trying to figure out what she could be thinking. He'd recognized her remorse and fear, could understand the depth of that fear more now. And it came to him then, as he cleared his windshield of sleet, that she was thinking more of him than of herself.

Yes, that had always been Cassie's way. She'd always looked out after Mike, Springer, Jesse, her own father—those she loved before herself.

She was afraid that her fear would hurt him. This thing will only bring you pain, she'd said. I won't let you do something you'll regret. She was not only dealing with her own distorted inner fear, but worrying about him, as well.

She'd kept this thing hidden from her brothers all these years, while it had eaten at her. Part of it, Quent was sure, was her pride. Cassie would rather die than admit such a flaw as fear. The Marlows were supposed to be a fearless breed. And, Quent admitted to himself, a lot of that stemmed from some overblown image men and women had of themselves out here in the rough-hewn land. The image had remained, handed down from generation to generation.

She'd hidden it because she hadn't wanted to worry or distress her brothers. They thought her strong and invincible—yet she was very human after all. They had been so preoccupied with their own lives that they'd just never seen it.

Ah, my Cassie, he thought, longing to comfort her.

No, he couldn't push her, Quent thought, but he could talk to her, lead her to think his way. He gave a large sigh, feeling as if he were thinking of attempting to change the color of the moon. But it was all the ammunition he had at the moment, and he wouldn't give up until he'd won.

The enormity of everything settled on him. Was it worth all this? Once again his ire rose as he remembered what she'd just done. "Damn fool woman," he muttered. Maybe she was right. Hell, he hadn't known Cassie to be wrong very often. He might be better off letting her go.

But he knew he couldn't. He was crazy, he decided. Yes, he was in love.

A bit of male egotism touched him, and even as he recognized the emotion for what it was, he half believed it. There hadn't been a woman yet whom he hadn't been able to sweet talk. And there was no doubting Cassie was one hell of a woman. He guessed he was up against the challenge of his life.

Cassie took sanctuary in her bedroom. She'd come straight home after her disastrous escapade at the Donner farm, forgetting all about picking up Jesse from the store. She didn't think of it until she heard him calling her name. Composing herself and gearing up her courage, she met him at the top of the stairway to apologize. She told him she didn't feel well, hoping that would pass as explanation for her red and swollen eyes. Judging by his expression, she doubted very much if it did.

That was all she could think of to say, and again she closed herself inside the bedroom. "Do your homework," she offered to Jesse through the door, verbally reaching out to him, feeling as if she were abandoning her brothers. She was always there to get their meals, make sure they had clothes for the following day and to just generally be there if they needed her.

Just for tonight, she told herself, guilt settling on her as she imagined the meal Springer and Jesse would scrounge for themselves.

How could she have done what she had? Cassie wondered and berated herself for the hundredth time. She hadn't even been truly thinking. She'd acted simply and totally on uncontrollable emotion. Quent had a perfect right to be infuriated with her. What a stupid, irrational thing for her to have done.

The scene came back to her in snatches, in living color: Springer behind the truck; the awful junky Donner yard; looking and not finding Quent, then finally seeing him behind the water trough.

Unexpectedly, like a fragment of light piercing her darkness, a chuckle started deep in the pit of her stomach and gradually forced its way up and out. How funny it seemed now in retrospect. Stupid, crazy, but yes, sort of funny, too. And no matter how irritated Quent was with her, he'd have to admit her action had gotten Orin Donner to come from the house all on his own, keeping everyone safe and sound. If she wanted to look at it in a prideful way, she'd done what two men had not been able to.

Pride, she thought with a shake of her head, she had a lot of it. So did Quent. She'd hurt him by her actions, butting into his world. It was better to end this now, before she could hurt him any further. The thought stabbed afresh into her heart, and she wondered how she could possibly feel any more pain in a heart that was surely already dead.

The darkness of sorrow surrounded her again, though she could think and see things more clearly now, and somehow even found a small shred of compassion for herself. She loved him; it would follow that she'd be afraid for him. And even if they could both manage to tame their prideful and willful natures, the fear would always be there. A fear to tear them apart.

At this moment, she could understand herself. She was a perfectly sensible woman, in control. It didn't seem possible that she, Cassie Marlow, could turn into that irrational, fear-controlled human being.

But yet it had happened. And when that fear rose, it was strong and real. She would have to face it, do her best to deal with it and not drag Quent into it with her weakness.

Chapter Thirteen

Knocking on her door woke Cassie. She blinked, realizing she'd dozed off, emotionally exhausted and drained. It was evening, only a bit before nine. The knocking came again, and she rose to answer it, preparing to assure Springer or Jesse that she was fine.

But when she opened the door, she looked up into Quent's eyes. Shock stopped her breath. He gave his mellow grin, though a twitch of his jaw betrayed his uncertainty.

"Springer knew I wanted to be alone." The words tangled with her tongue as she took a step backward.

"He gave me his blessing," Quent said, stepping into the room. He seemed to fill it.

She swallowed, backing up until she bumped into the bedstead. "I said all I had to say this afternoon."

"You did," Quent said in a low tone, "but I didn't." His eyes flickered over her quickly, but long enough to remind her that she wore only a robe.

Quent saw the questioning flit across Cassie's face. She looked like a frightened doe before him, her chest rapidly rising and falling, her eyes so wide and round. Quent wanted to reach out to her, the threat of losing her fueling his rising desire. It tore at him; he wanted to wipe away the hurt and fear. But he didn't advance any closer, and he searched carefully for his words.

"This is hardly fair," she said, regarding him warily. "I'm in my robe."

"Oh? What's unfair about it?"

"I have a feeling we are about to argue, and wearing a robe hardly gives a woman confidence."

"You want me to leave so you can change?"

She nodded.

He started to comply, then halted and turned back to her. "I don't think so. Trying to talk to you through a locked door would hardly give me confidence." By the look on her face he knew he'd guessed right, and a speck of wry admiration touched him. She'd been trying to maneuver him right out of the room, and had not intended to open the door again.

She frowned. "I'm listening." Averting her eyes, she stiffened her shoulders, as if preparing for an assault.

"I love you, for starters. I was angry this afternoon, and I think we both said a few things we didn't mean." He waited for a reaction. There was none. "But I meant it when I said I understood," he continued, "and I wanted to repeat that now when you've had time to cool off."

"I heard you this afternoon." She raised her eyes to him, those wide heart-wrenching eyes. "But I don't think you can possibly understand. And maybe I didn't make myself clear. I don't want this relationship to go any further. I'm not going to change my mind." Her chin jutted out slightly.

He looked at her for a moment. "Is that what you really want, Cassie?" The question hung there between them.

"Yes." Her voice was a hoarse whisper.

Her eyes wavered a fraction; that was all. For the first time doubt seeped into Quent. Could it be that was what she truly wanted? His gaze moved to her mouth, and he remembered her lips as they'd looked that very afternoon after he'd been kissing her. Surely she couldn't have changed her feelings so much in the hours since, no matter what had happened.

"Suppose you enumerate your reasons," he said. He stood very still, his gaze pointedly holding hers. If he had to corner her to get her to see this problem in a true light, he would.

She took a breath, and Quent could practically see her mind working. "I don't think I have to," she said finally, annoyance tracing her voice.

Quent's ire rose. She was just being stubborn! Then he quickly banked the emotion. He wasn't going to get anywhere unless he could stay calm. Idly he moved to the window, relaxing his muscles.

"Mike and I did some talking, a lot of remembering, when he was here," he said. "What you said about your mother watching the window—well, yes, she did. And Cassie, I know it's hard to hear, but she had her problems."

"I know about my mother, Quent," Cassie said in a low voice. "I lived here, too."

"What you saw of her—it wasn't just her body that was weak, Cass." Quent spoke gently. "It was her mind, too. She was overly emotional about everything. She—"

Cassie cut him off. "I know, Quent. And I also know I was affected by her reactions, and by my father's attempts to deal with her, but he never could. I can see this thing quite clearly. That's not the problem. The fear is still with me. I've tried dealing with it. I will deal with it. And one of the surest ways is to not put myself into a position where I am constantly thrown up against it. And no matter what the cause, it would be there, and would always stand between us. There could be other scenes like this afternoon. I could never promise there wouldn't be."

He'd always hated it when Cassie talked like this, so cool, calm, logical. She did truly know, he saw, and it took the wind out of him. It had been his hope to show her the possible root of her fear, show her how distorted and needless it was, and that doing so would enable her to conquer it. He should have known that though the emotion was irrational, she would have quite rationally figured it all out.

Irritation tugged at him, and he raked a hand through his hair. "Okay, so you've got it all figured out. But this one time you're wrong, Cassie. We can make it—and make it good, if you'd just give us half a chance. And I know you're thinking a lot about how this could affect me, but could you just have some faith in me?" He saw a flash of reaction. "Did you ever think of it that way? That you're not having faith in me? What do you know of me, Cass? Do you think so little of me that you think I can't handle something like this? I'm not your father—and I don't mean to put him down at all. But I'm not him. And you're not your mother. We are us. And I happen to think we're pretty terrific. And I love you. And by God, I've never said that to another woman."

Confusion was etched in her face. "I—" She shook her head.

Quent sensed he'd hit his mark. "Cassie..." As he moved to touch her, she pivoted away, turning her back to him, but he continued. "Cassie, I am all those things you think I am—rowdy, sometimes downright irresponsible, and I guess a bit of a flirt. But I do have it in me to love you—a love for now, forever. Come what may. And I'll guarantee you'll never be bored with me." He paused, searching for a reaction, but finding none. He walked to the door. "You think about what I've said. I'll call you tomorrow."

Just as he was about to step into the hall, Cassie spoke. "I've told you my decision. I won't change my mind."

He didn't call. Cassie found herself listening for the telephone, and disappointment that she tried to deny tugged at her. It was for the best, she affirmed to herself. And why should he call after what she'd told him? She'd meant what she'd said, and once she'd made up her mind, she wasn't easily inclined to change it.

Christmas came and went. Mike returned home only for Christmas Eve to leave again late afternoon on Christmas day; it appeared he'd found another special girl over in Reno. It snowed, a very wet and heavy snow that painted the world a fluffy white before it melted again two days later.

The weather grew mild, and Jesse spent a lot of time riding his three-wheeler, geering up for competition in the spring. Springer was away often, too, and Cassie suspected some special investigation. When she asked him about it, he told her of the large-scale deer poaching operation Quent had mentioned earlier. Springer told her it baffled him that he wasn't able to locate something so large as a tractor-trailer truck, but the back roads were numerous, with only a handful of rangers to cover them.

Several times Cassie thought she heard a helicopter over the house. Once she saw one, but it was too far away to see if it was Quent. One time she saw his truck pass by on the road out front. Going to the Snowden house, she knew. The Hatfield house, she repeated sadly to herself.

Memories of him, the golden light in his eyes, his smile, the very scent of him, came unbidden to her thoughts, sneaking in as a thief to steal any remnant of peace of mind she could recover.

What Quent had said that evening in her bedroom stayed with her, growing as a tiny seed planted in dark moist soil struggles for sunlight. Was it lack of faith in him? Perhaps, though it went against the grain to admit it, there was much truth in what he'd said. She hadn't looked at it as lack of faith in him, but in herself. Would he really be able to make a difference in her handling of the fear? More and more she longed to find out, to give in and take the strength and comfort he was offering. *But what would happen if he couldn't handle it, if he were wrong?*

The second day of the new year Cassie passed the Doyle City police station on her way from visiting Anita. Instinctively, before she could think, her eyes were drawn to seek Quent's helicopter. It was there, with Quent beside it, tools strewn at his feet. As if impelled by a magnet, Cassie pulled her truck to the side of the road. He had his back to her and he didn't turn around. Her heart pounded as she looked at him, wanting so much to go to him. What would it hurt?

"Oh!" she muttered aloud to herself, shifting into gear and pulling away. How could she even have thought such a thing?

At that moment she saw the days before her quite clearly. They stretched endlessly, lifelessly. It was a bleak, almost unbearable realization.

She was so afraid of hurt that she was building a life for herself devoid of any feeling at all. No hurt or sadness, but completely barren of joy, as well. Because it took both to make a life. One simply couldn't be had without the other. Together, they were life.

Quent called only a few minutes after she'd entered the feed store.

"I saw you," he said.

Her heart pounded. She allowed herself a tiny glimmer of pleasure. It felt good. "Yes?" she said.

"I want to see you." His mellow voice had a tense questioning edge.

"Yes." The word had flowed from her lips.

She could practically see his smile. "I'll be over tonight after dinner." Eagerness had warmed his voice.

"I'd—I'd like that," she said hesitantly. She held the receiver for a long minute after Quent had hung up, wondering if she had just thrown away every shred of common sense. But at least she was feeling again. Fear? Yes, she did feel her old enemy fear, but she felt an enormous amount of anticipation and joy, as well.

In her mind she heard again his strong, sure voice. Quentin Hatfield, she thought, was the strongest man she'd ever known. A warm sense of security came with the thought.

She left the store early, eager to get home and dress in something special. But dinner was interrupted by a telephone call. Springer answered, and listening to his few terse words, Cassie knew Quent wouldn't be coming.

"Quent says he'll call as soon as he can, no matter what time it is," Springer told her after he'd hung up and as he reached for his gun on the top of the refrigerator. "We've got a line on those guys with the truck we've been after."

Cassie's stomach did a somersault, cold dread shooting down her spine as her gaze rested on the gun at Springer's hip. But it wasn't Springer's gun she saw. It was Quent's. Her gaze moved back up to Springer's face, trying to imprint his image in her mind.

Springer looked at her; then his gaze moved sharply to Jesse. "Stay home with Cassie tonight," he said.

"Aw, some of the guy—" Jesse broke off, glancing from Springer to Cassie. "Yeah. There's a good race on TV tonight."

Cassie didn't say anything. While still tugging his coat over his uniform, Springer sprinted out the door. She watched from the window as he drove away. Night was setting in, and the sky to the west was barely a cream color now.

She did the dishes, and amazingly Jesse helped, then she shooed him off to watch television in the living room. She sat in the rocker. Cork came to lay his head on her knee, and she stroked his thick coat.

She should do something, she thought, to occupy her mind. So she called Anita and spoke for a few minutes, not telling her friend about what was happening. Then she tried to watch television with Jesse, tried to work on a cross-stitch and finally ended up back in the kitchen, baking cookies.

The time dragged on, and all the while Cassie battled the demon fear. *Where were they? What was happening? Were they using guns?*

She considered calling Hadley Smith's wife, or another of the wives she knew to try to find out something, but they wouldn't know any more than she did. She had the insane desire to drive out and look for them, but she couldn't go running out there the way she'd done before, she told herself firmly. For heaven's sake, she scolded herself, they could be two counties away.

She'd simply have to wait.

Jesse fell asleep during the late show, and Cassie covered him up there on the couch. She ate nearly a dozen of her fresh-baked cookies, then began to walk through the dimly lit house. She stood for a brief moment looking out of Springer's window into the back meadow. Moonlight flooded the earth. She wondered if this would be a help or a hindrance for the men.

Horrible pictures flashed through her mind, distorted visions of Quent hurt and bleeding in the moonlight, and Springer, too. Folding her arms, she hugged them to herself, her body actually aching with tension that alternated with hot flashes and cold chills. She tried to block out the distorted images of fear, but they repeatedly returned to taunt her, to pound at her, to hold her in their remorseless grip.

Suddenly the telephone rang. Cassie jumped, icy fingers of fear mixed with tingles of hope shooting down her back. She raced through the darkened dining room, tripping over the rug, and reached breathlessly for the telephone in the brightly lit kitchen.

"Hello," she answered breathlessly.

The line buzzed, but no one spoke.

"Hello," she repeated more loudly, her heart pounding.

Cassie let out a long sigh, her spirit shriveling. A wrong number. Oh, Lord, what a night to get a stupid wrong number. Her gaze moved to the clock. It was past one.

The tears bubbled up in her eyes and coursed down her face. It just hurt so badly, and she was so tired. "How dare this happen," she raged aloud in a hoarse whisper. Then she pleaded wordlessly, *please, God, let them come home*.

A half an hour later the telephone rang again. Cassie ran to it just as quickly as before, her heart pounding, but lifted the receiver hesitantly, fearing both to hear and not to hear.

"Cassie?" Springer said. "Are you there?"

"Yes." Immense relief flooded her. "Oh, Springer are you all right? How is Quent? Let me talk to him." She couldn't wait to hear his voice.

"He can't right this minute." Springer paused. "His father's patching him up. He's been hurt, but not bad, Cass. Don't get upset. We just wanted to call and let you know we're okay."

She could barely get her breath. "What's happened to him? Where is he? Is he at the hospital?" she fired the questions at him, her mind racing ahead, calculating the time it would take her to drive to the hospital.

"No, he's here at his father's clinic," Springer said. "We were closer to here. He's going to be fine, Cass," he repeated.

"I'll be there in ten minutes," she spoke into the phone, hearing Springer call after her even as she hung up. She had to see Quent, had to make sure for herself that he was all right.

In less than ten minutes Springer led Cassie to a treatment room at Dr. Tom's clinic, repeating over and over that Quent was fine, has just been grazed by a shot. Cassie's mind echoed with the word: *shot, shot, shot.*

Quent sat upon the table while his father wrapped a bandage around his shoulder. Cassie just stood there looking at him, angry, fearful, relieved. Quent looked up to see her, and she saw the pain in his eyes. Neither of them said anything.

Dr. Tom glanced at both of them over the rim of his glasses. "I'll leave you two alone for a few minutes, but whatever you have to say, you'd better get to it. Your mother, Quent, will not be put off from seeing you much longer."

As Dr. Tom pulled the door shut behind him, Cassie stepped hesitantly over to Quent, her gaze remaining steadily on his. His good arm went out and caught her to him, and she pressed her face to his bare chest. The tears came then, beginning softly, then turning into hard sobs. Quent held her, saying nothing.

She tried to stop crying, tried to say something, but she knew her words were unintelligible. She wanted to tell him she was okay. She wanted to tell him not to worry about her.

But of course all that was a lie. She wasn't okay. The man she loved had just been shot.

Quent just held her pressed against him. He said not one word. He didn't tell her it didn't matter. He didn't press platitudes on her that she couldn't believe. He simply held her, tightly, strongly.

Gradually she felt his quiet strength generating to her. He could handle it, he'd told her, and he was. In his quiet, mellow way.

Tentatively she reached out to touch the large bandage covering his shoulder, then moved her fingers to stroke his taut cheek.

Quent sighed. "I guess it's no use telling you this was some sort of fluke. That this much rarely happens to a ranger in a year, much less the space of weeks." He gave a crooked, bitter smile, avoiding her gaze.

"Quent," Cassie said softly. "I love you."

He looked at her, his brows knotted as he studied her. "What are you saying?"

"That I love you, Quentin Hatfield. And if you still want me, then I'll marry you."

He looked as if he couldn't quite understand what she'd said. "Tonight—you've been terrified," he said, the words a statement and a question.

Cassie nodded. "I've eaten myself into another dress size, then couldn't eat at all, and then walked ruts in the floor." Again she touched his cheek, marveling that she could touch him, could see him. "Oh, Quent, I've been so worried about you and Springer. Thank God you're safe."

With his good arm, Quent held her to him, murmuring into her hair, "I'm sorry, Cass." He tilted her head so she'd look at him, devouring her with his eyes. "Then why, Cassie? Why have you decided to marry me now?"

"Don't you want me?" she asked, giving a low chuckle.

"Hell, yes, I do," he swore vehemently. His gaze narrowed. "But you answer me. Don't tell me the sight of me trussed up like this has weakened you. That will only last a few days, and then you'll regret it."

Cassie smiled gently, brushing the tears from her eyes so she could see more clearly. "You do look pitiful." She shook her head. "But it's not that." She brushed his lips with a soft kiss, then looked full into his eyes. "I learned something today, and all during this horrible night. I learned that you can't live without loving, and that loving means giving of yourself, which involves pain and fear, but also joy and pleasure. I thought about what you said about believing in you. I do, Quent. If any man is man enough to put up with me, I guess it's you."

A warm light came into his eyes. "Oh, you think so?"

"I'm banking on it," she said; then she searched his face. "But I can't promise not to run out to find you or not to do something else equally as foolish."

He regarded her tenderly. "We'll handle it, Cass. Together."

Joy slipped into her heart. "I learned something else tonight, too," she said quietly. "And it may sound a bit cold and unromantic, but I learned I'm not going to die if something happens to you. I may have to deal with a lot of fear, maybe even the pain of loss, but it's all a part of life—and I'll not die from it. I'll live. And while I'm living, I'll experience an awful lot of joy and pleasure. Especially with you."

Quent just sat there, as if digesting her words. "Won't die without me, huh?" he asked in gentle mock outrage. "What kind of romantic thing is that to tell a suffering man?"

In answer Cassie gave him a deliberately sensuous smile and traced a fingernail down the middle of his chest.

At that moment the door burst open, and Marjean Hatfield walked in. "Oh," she said, glancing at the two of them standing so close. She pressed her lips tightly. "I think you need to get into bed now, son," she said, "and your father needs his sleep too. He's ready to give you another pain shot before we all retire."

"Yes, Mom." Quent moved his shoulder, wincing as he did. "And I could use another shot. But Mom," he said gently, "I'm going home with Cassie. She's said she'll marry me, and I'm not letting her out of my sight until she does."

Cassie started and looked at Marjean, and just then Springer appeared in the doorway. "Everything okay in here?" His voice trailed off, his gaze moving around everyone.

Marjean gave a slight nod, sparing Cassie a tight smile. "You'll call me in the morning?" she asked Quent.

"Of course he will," Cassie assured her. Quent smiled, his gaze only for her.

Later, Cassie lay in her darkened bedroom, her head in the crook of Quent's good arm. She hadn't wanted to lie against him for fear of hurting him, but, his speech slurred, he'd insisted, saying he'd had plenty of pain medication and couldn't feel a thing. And he didn't like it, he complained as he tried to fondle her breast through her soft gown just before he fell into a deep drugged sleep.

Smiling with contentment, Cassie gently moved away to look at him. The bright moon bathed the room with silver light, enough to see the outline of his face. She smoothed his brow with a fingertip, love welling up and filling her heart to bursting. She marveled at the emotion and the sensations it caused. She'd never felt such joy and contentment in all her life. Tonight she had experienced the pain of fear and dread, the breathlessness that comes with relief, and the indescribable warm joy that comes with loving. She was very much alive.

As she drifted into a peaceful sleep, she thought of the days and nights to come, and the fearful shadows fell behind her.

COMING NEXT MONTH

ALL OR NOTHING—Brittany Young
Christa and Matteo were in love, with plans for the future. Then Matteo's brother died, leaving him with family responsibilities—responsibilities that included a fiancée.

MOONLIGHT BANDIT—Stella Bagwell
Could a high-fashion model from New York make it in down home Texas *and* take care of a little girl? R.J. didn't think so, but Maggie was determined to prove him wrong.

HEAVENLY BODIES—Pepper Adams
Music teacher Cody Dalton fell in love with Spence DeHaven when she blundered into the men's room. When the heavenly astronomer didn't respond to her charms, she teamed with his daughters to bring him down to earth.

MAVERICK—Jennifer Mikels
Someone was sabotaging the neighboring ranches, and Carrie was determined to find out who. Matt was just as determined . . . to make her his wife.

A BETTER MAN—Brenda Trent
Grant's brother was a bum! Why else would he hurt a lovely woman like Kimberly? Wanting to help, Grant invited her to his home to recover. And promptly fell in love.

SWEET HOMECOMING—Emilie Richards
Jennifer was a MacDonald, loyal to her family. But now the bank was foreclosing on their farm. She had one last chance to save it. Rusk said he loved her—but could she trust him? Or would they lose everything?

AVAILABLE THIS MONTH:

FAMILY AFFAIR
Rita Rainville

GIFT OF THE GODS
Judith McWilliams

A MAN FOR SYLVIA
Sue Santore

THE FOREVER KIND
Karen Young

FOR EACH TOMORROW
Curtiss Ann Matlock

NO QUESTIONS ASKED
Lynnette Morland

ATTRACTIVE, SPACE SAVING BOOK RACK

Display your most prized novels on this handsome and sturdy book rack. The hand-rubbed walnut finish will blend into your library decor with quiet elegance, providing a practical organizer for your favorite hard-or soft-covered books.

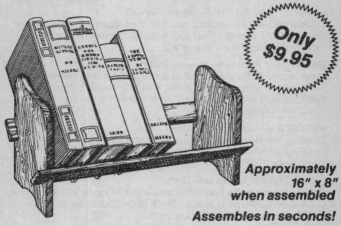

Only $9.95

Approximately 16" x 8" when assembled

Assembles in seconds!

To order, rush your name, address and zip code, along with a check or money order for $10.70* ($9.95 plus 75¢ postage and handling) payable to *Silhouette Books*.

Silhouette Books
Book Rack Offer
901 Fuhrmann Blvd.
P.O. Box 1325
Buffalo, NY 14269-1325

Offer not available in Canada.

*New York residents add appropriate sales tax.

BKR-2R

Take 4 Silhouette
Special Edition novels
FREE

and preview future books in your home for 15 days!

When you take advantage of this offer, you get 4 Silhouette Special Edition® novels FREE and without obligation. Then you'll also have the opportunity to preview 6 brand-new books —delivered right to your door for a FREE 15-day examination period—as soon as they are published.

When you decide to keep them, you pay just $1.95 each ($2.50 each in Canada) *with no shipping, handling, or other charges of any kind!*

Romance *is* alive, well and flourishing in the moving love stories of Silhouette Special Edition novels. They'll awaken your desires, enliven your senses, and leave you tingling all over with excitement... and the first 4 novels are yours to keep. You can cancel at any time.

As an added bonus, you'll also receive a FREE subscription to the Silhouette Books Newsletter as long as you remain a member. Each issue is filled with news on upcoming books, interviews with your favorite authors, even their favorite recipes.

To get your 4 FREE books, fill out and mail the coupon today!

Silhouette Special Edition®

Silhouette Books, 120 Brighton Rd., P.O. Box 5084, Clifton, NJ 07015-5084